BUCKSKINNER

AN EVANS NOVEL OF THE WEST

R. C. HOUSE

BUCKSKINNER

M. EVANS AND COMPANY, INC.
NEW YORK

M. Evans and Company, Inc.
216 East 49th Street
New York, New York 10017

Library of Congress Cataloging-in-Publication Data

House, R. C.
    Buckskinner / R.C. House. — 1st ed.
        p. cm. — (An Evans novel of the West)
    Sequel to: Warhawk.
    ISBN 0-87131-783-4 (cl) : $19.95
    I. Title. II. Series.
PS3558.0864B8   1995
813'.54—dc20   94-49020
                                                          CIP

Typeset by Classic Type, Inc.

Manufactured in the United States of America

First Edition

9 8 7 6 5 4 3 2 1

Dedicated to my cherished

BOBKAT

Bob and Kathy Hellman

The Best of the Buckskinners

For love and caring from

Those early rendezvous to Capitan!

Historical Note

MAJOR EVENTS IN THE LIVES OF DR. MARCUS WHITMAN and his wife related in this story are basically factual. Dr. Whitman and the sometimes irascible Rev. Samuel Parker joined the American Fur Company wagon train led by Lucien Fontenelle, bound for the 1835 mountain-man rendezvous on the Green River in what is now Wyoming. They were tormented and taunted by their rude and discourteous traveling companions until Dr. Whitman heroically saved a great number of lives when the crew was stricken with cholera. It is also a well-known mountain-man legend that at the 1835 rendezvous on New Fork of the Green, Dr. Whitman removed—without anesthetic—the arrowhead long embedded in Jim Bridger's back.

While Rev. Parker proceeded to Oregon to establish a Christian mission among the Indians, Dr. Whitman returned east to marry his Narcissa and bring her west the following year, along with Rev. Henry Spalding and his wife, Eliza. History tells us that they were the first white women to venture so far west (though this book fictionally speculates that Rachel Lyman had been west of the Continental Divide for some years). Narcissa—and to some measure, Eliza—charmed celebrants at the 1836 fur-trade rendezvous, including Bridger and another celebrated mountain man, Joe Meek (both of whom in later years were to turn over half-breed daughters to the Whitmans to care for and educate). The missionaries'

1

reception at the mountain men's 1836 Horse Creek rendezvous was about as portrayed—the preliminary shivaree
two days' travel from rendezvous, as well as the enthusiastic
welcome at rendezvous proper. Mrs. Whitman's record of the
events remarks on her emotions as an Indian "chief" (could it
have been Walking Feather and Moon-That-Grows?) deco-
rously introduced her to his wife.

Rev. Spalding's cantankerous behavior is well-documented
as stemming from an unrequited love of Narcissa Prentiss.

The 1837 smallpox epidemic among the Indian tribes of
the upper Missouri began and progressed with the level of
catastrophe about as described. This fictional account, if
anything, minimizes the extent of the horrors experienced by
the vulnerable western tribes.

In Oregon, Marcus and the beautiful and charming
Narcissa developed their medical and educational mission
among the Cayuse Indians at Waiilatpu near present-day
Walla Walla, Washington.

The accidental death of the Whitman's only child—their
beloved two-year-old Alice Clarissa—was as related to Jake
Lyman by Jim Bridger.

An epilogue further details the lives—and the deaths—of
Dr. Marcus and Narcissa Whitman.

1835

Chapter One

SUN'S FIRST LIGHT BROKE OVER THE EASTERN RIDGE WITH THE explosive glory of resurrection, but the faint odor reaching Jake Lyman's nose was of death—the foul, sick stench that seeps out with the agony of lingering, fatal suffering.

Rachel reined her horse closer to Jake's, her face tight with concern; he was sure she hadn't yet smelled it as strongly as he. They were still more than a quarter-mile off.

"Something's wrong down there, Jake" she said. "I don't know what, but I can feel it. Something's not right."

"I've a hunch there's sickness in that wagon circle yonder. We'd best stay back. Where people gather in so close, illness can run roughshod. Epidemic."

For the moment, they rested their horses on the grassy slope, high up and west of the circled wagons, studying, trying to understand, and sifting options.

Rachel spoke softly. "We might be needed, Jake."

The train, Lyman could have seen with half an eye, had been stalled for several days. The wagons had been circled in orderly fashion; the horse and mule herd corralled inside had cropped the grass to bare dirt. Lyman could see that the animals needed a fresh area to graze and probably should be taken to water; the Missouri River was close by.

But there were more compelling needs; outside the wagons' perimeter as many as fifteen men sprawled like corpses on buffalo robes, India-rubber rain ponchos, and blankets aligned in almost organized rows. Paths between them had been trampled through the golden, cured grass.

"Trail sickness, I'm thinkin'," Jacob Lyman murmured, repeating himself in his concern. He spoke so low that Rachel scarcely heard him as he tried to fathom the scene below. "The kind that spreads when people live tight together. And kills. Smallpox, maybe. Or the cholera."

He could see two men moving among the rows of the ailing, here and there bending over to care for one of them. Some distance away, over a deep bed of smoldering, untended buffalo chips, a black wide and shallow iron pot, steaming with hot water, hung suspended from an iron-rod tripod. Other cookware was snugged up to the fire's rim to keep warm—a coffee pot, maybe, and other smaller black iron vessels likely containing nutritional soups, stews, and medicinal teas.

Still farther from the rows of the makeshift hospital, beside a small white canvas wall tent, a man in a suit of fine black broadcloth and a buttoned white shirt without a tie, sat reading a black-bound book in a folding camp chair of wood, metal brackets, and canvas. His once blond hair was thinning and fading to white. Lyman sensed an air about the man from his rigid posture that he'd have little to do with the crisis raging a short distance from him.

To his right, Jacob saw Daniel on horseback emerge over a grass-choked rise. He waved to his foster son with a beckoning gesture. Around the lad's horse, the tall and sere stalks of golden grass flowed in a slight breeze like ripples on a good-sized lake. Eager for adventure, Rachel's eighteen-year-old had been allowed to explore the land through which they traveled, warned not to venture too far; hostile Indians also laid certain claim to these lands.

Always—and sadly—appalled by the arrogance and indifference of many whites toward the Indians, Lyman knew that despite his own respect and acceptance of Indian ways, his white skin marked him as suspect, if not an outright enemy. He knew that because of his feelings and actions, he enjoyed a broad respect wherever Indians encountered white beaver trappers. Still, a great many Indians might not have heard of Jacob Lyman; in this country, white men—and red—rode with one eye on their back trail. Every stranger was suspect until proven otherwise.

Lyman watched with a glow of pride as Daniel, dressed in the fringed buckskins of a free trapper, led his horse in an easy canter to join them. The boy rode well. Little was visible of the defeated, sullen slouch that characterized the Daniel England that Lyman rescued from his evil white mentors eight months back. Now his shoulders were squared, his back straight but flexible, his head up, alert and inquisitive. Aside from an occasional lapse into his old pattern of unreasonable behavior and furies, the boy had adjusted well. Life with Jacob and Rachel, Daniel's mother—with whom Lyman had managed a reunion after their five-year separation as Indian captives—was controlled and disciplined in comparison to the past.

In minutes, Daniel's horse reached them and the three clustered on the grassy slope overlooking the mysterious wagon camp spread below.

"What's it about, Jacob?" Daniel asked. Though Rachel referred to him affectionately as Jake, Lyman demanded the boy's respect in calling him by his full name, Jacob. Apart from that, Lyman, as foster father, judiciously meted out Daniel's freedoms and informalities, holding back more than he allowed. After the lad's five missing adolescent years as an Indian captive and later as a depraved renegade, it would take a lot of grooming before all the snags and snarls were curried out of him. Still, Lyman saw in the boy more cultured flowers than ugly weeds.

"Fur company pack train bound for rendezvous, Daniel. No question. Loaded with trade goods from St. Louis. Headed for the Green River rendezvous next month—the one I hope we get back to after we attend to our own personal affairs, and, I suppose, after we help out down there. Even from here, I take one of the men on their feet to be old Lucien Fontenelle, looking after those on the ground, sick with some sort of plague. So it's an American Fur Company train bound for the '35 rendezvous on Green River. Fontenelle's lately thrown in with Tom Fitzpatrick and Milton Sublette and Jim Bridger in the fur business. It's critical that those wagons get there in time for the first trading and, by the looks, Lucien's way behind schedule. In serious trouble. I don't know the other man with Lucien taking care of the sick. Nor can I make out the old man sitting off away there reading by the canvas tent. Strange."

"Want me to ride down there and ask, Jacob?" Daniel asked, eagerness shown in his eyes.

Lyman smiled at the young man he hoped one day to be able properly to call son. "No, Daniel. We'll go down to a respectful and safe distance and find out what we can. If we can help without jeopardizing ourselves, we will. Otherwise, despicable as it is, it may be best all-around for us to ride on."

Rachel glared at him, bristled and spoke up. "Jake, if the sick are not properly or sufficiently cared for—and out here I can't see how they could be—we have a duty here. To do something. Unless there is a doctor there, the care those men get is rough and rude. There must be ways for us to ease their miseries. We'll not ride away until we've determined what those ways might be."

Lyman laid a comforting, understanding hand on the arm of the woman he loved and accepted as wife, though their union had yet to be sanctified in the eyes of God and under the laws of man. Lyman smiled at her affectionately and indulgently. She was a woman of deep, abiding loves and compassion—and passions. Otherwise, he would not have been attracted to her.

"We'll not ride on, Rachel dear, until I'm fully assured there's no need of our help. Or serious hazard."

Lyman caught a suspicious—possibly jealous—glint in Daniel's eye as he studied Lyman and his closeness to his mother; the boy still hadn't fully accepted Lyman's role as his mother's chosen replacement for Daniel's long-dead father. Despite all he and the boy had been through, Lyman knew he still had a long, uphill battle to win the lad's complete confidence and trust.

"Nothing to be gained up here," Lyman said. "Let's ride down and inquire. There may be less chance of being tainted if we speak first with the man at the tent. He appears the most hale and hearty."

Lyman urged his horse downslope, favoring a course away from the circled wagons and toward the solitary tent, aloof in its distance from the emergency. Side by side, Rachel and Daniel steered their horses after him. As they rode toward it, Fontenelle's companion in the camp of the stricken saw the course of the three approaching riders. He spoke something quickly to Fontenelle, broke away from tending the sick and strode out to intercept them.

Lyman steered their course back toward the wagons and held up his hand for Rachel and Daniel to halt. "Let me go on in and learn what I can. You stay back. If there's contagion, there's no sense in our all being exposed."

Understanding, Rachel and Daniel reined their horses without a word. Lyman left his horse with them.

The man walking to meet him, Lyman judged, was younger than he, maybe by a half-dozen years; early thirties, Lyman figured. He wore the buckskin garb of a trapper, but the 'skins were new and well-made. He had the strong, stocky build of a man normally in robust good health. Lyman could also see—in the sag of his body and his drawn, ashen complexion—that he was not only exhausted but probably suffering a touch of the malady that brought the westbound wagons to a standstill. Beneath the man's stooped posture and sickly pallor, Lyman also saw evidence of decency, drive, and dedication. The man waved Lyman to a stop a ways off, only close enough for them to communicate over the distance in loud tones.

"Asiatic cholera," he called in a strained voice. "You and your people must stay back."

"I have no notion of doing otherwise," Lyman answered, trying to smile to ease a tense situation.

"Best you ride on," the man called. "Every one of the train's workmen is down with the sickness. It is wildly contagious. Mr. Fontenelle and I suffer mild cases, and are only on our feet because we must be. I don't need any more patients."

"I read the sign of your predicament from the hill," Lyman responded. "Lucien Fontenelle and I are well acquainted. We want to help."

"Everything's being done that is humanly possible. I shan't risk anyone else being taken down. I will tell Lucien of your concern. Your name?"

Jake observed that the man was businesslike to the point of being brusque. "Lyman," he responded "Jacob Lyman. A free trapper. That is, not employed in Mr. Fontenelle's company." Though the man before him seemed competent, Lyman sensed from his bearing and from his language that he knew little of fur-hunting activities or of the West of the Shinin' Mountains.

"Lucien knows me," Lyman continued. "We're bound east on business . . . me, my intended wife and her son. Don't know as I've seen you before."

"With good reason." The stranger almost bowed. "Forgive me. I forget my manners in the face of our crisis and so far from genteel society. And for want of rest and suffering a touch of their symptoms. My first trip west. The name's Whitman; Dr. Marcus Whitman, medical missionary sponsored by the American Board of Foreign Missions. Bound for the Oregon country. The Reverend Samuel Parker, by the tent yonder, and I joined Mr. Fontenelle's caravan in St. Louis to travel in its security to the Green River summer encampment. I must say, we were treated shabbily by Fontenelle's men as unwelcome nuisances. That was before

I stepped in to care for their illnesses." Whitman smiled thinly. "Now they're grateful. Extremely so!"

"Rendezvous," Lyman corrected. "You say the man in the black suit yonder is a preacher?" He asked it eagerly.

"Yes. A good man, a decent and Christian man. But he fears that if he was taken with the rampant sickness, it might hinder, affect, or terminate his mission to bring the word of God to the Cayuse and Nez Perce. He distanced himself from the rest. With my blessing and understanding."

"But, I take it," Lyman said almost caustically, "the same principle doesn't apply to you." In Jake Lyman's West, when such crises arose, everyone turned to and helped.

"He is a man of God with a Bible. I am a man of God with a doctor's bag. I must get back, Mr. Lyman."

"I'm curious, Dr. Whitman, and forgive my forthrightness. Wouldn't a man of God with a Bible want to be among the sick and dying bringing words of strength and hope from the Almighty?"

Dr. Whitman, who had half-turned to go back to his duties among the sick, swung around. A small, twisted grin broke his fatigue-tight face. Lyman suspected a bit of impishness in the expression and was inwardly encouraged. "The Reverend Parker is a rather stern man, and I trust you will understand the word, pragmatic. Now, you must excuse me, Mr. Lyman."

"Only one more question, Dr. Whitman. Does your Reverend Parker perform marriages?"

"Of course. But you'll have to speak with him. I'll warn you that he appears gruff. His motives are righteous."

Lyman brightened. "Then I'm as far east as I need to go. My intended and I and her son will go into camp a safe distance. If you need anything, fresh meat, anything I can do, you just signal. I'll ask Reverend Parker to perform a wedding for Rachel and me after your crisis has passed and things around here even out. When we have time, I'll explain our circumstances."

Dr. Whitman's smile was now intense and genuine, and Lyman felt he saw a glint of new sparkle in the doctor's eyes. He surely stood more erect with his shoulders squared.

"We could use fresh meat, Mr. Lyman. And it will be great comfort to have someone else to call upon. I still insist you stay a safe distance to avoid contagion."

Dr. Whitman's eyes drifted to where Rev. Parker still sat solemnly reading his Bible beside the white canvas wall tent. "He hasn't been much help, Mr. Lyman," the doctor said, almost as a confession. Or perhaps as an apology.

"I suspected as much, Dr. Whitman. By the way, I go by Jake."

Hope continued its beam in Marcus Whitman's eyes. "Now I must get back to my patients. My good friends call me Mark, Jake. I hope you won't stand too long on formality."

"I've not been known to, Mark. We will speak again," Lyman said, turning to go back to Rachel and Daniel.

"I'll look forward to that, Jake," Whitman said as he turned and strode resolutely back towards his patients.

An afterthought caused Lyman to call after him. "Oh, Dr. Whitman?" The doctor also turned, smiling, seeming to welcome the delays in getting back to his demanding tasks caring for the sick. Lyman sensed that Whitman gained relief from being away from the constant crisis for a change.

"Jake?"

"You can tell Lucien that if I can persuade Reverend Parker to marry us, we'll ride back to rendezvous with the train and can hunt or help in other ways."

"He'll be heartened, Jake. If I can persuade him to stay away from his precious jug. I, myself, will surely look forward to it as well! Now, Jake, duty calls."

Chapter Two

IN ANTICIPATION OF STAYING PUT FOR A WHILE, RACHEL AND Daniel dismounted when Jake went to speak with Dr. Whitman. He strode back to where they waited, a safe distance away, holding the reins of their three saddle horses and two pack mounts with their camp and travel gear.

"Marvelous news, Rachel!" Jake called, coming up to them.

Her pretty, sun-darkened face studied him quizzically. Rachel's intensely black hair was parted in the middle, Indian-style, with braids plaited down both sides of her neck for ease and comfort while they traveled. In Lyman's eyes, she was beautiful. But strong-minded. "Men are deathly ill down there and you have wonderful news?"

Lyman chuckled. "I don't mean it that way, Rachel. Dr. Whitman, the man I spoke with, says it's Asiatic cholera. Deadly. Even he and Mr. Fontenelle are ill, but have to keep going to save the rest. As for us, it's just that we needn't go any farther east. The man by the tent yonder is an ordained preacher. Bound, Whitman says, for the Oregon country to establish Christian missions for the Indians. When things calm down, I'll get him to perform a proper ceremony for us."

Rachel smiled at him. "Now your enthusiasm makes sense, Jake. I'm gladdened." Lyman heard that well remembered tinkle of delight he found so precious in her voice. "Not only because at last we can be married. Travel across the plains is tedious and tiring. We'll get back home sooner. That's the most welcome news."

"This is poor country for a settled camp, Jacob," Daniel observed; at eighteen he sounded like a several-season hivernant mountain man which, Lyman acknowledged, Daniel probably was. He had certainly learned to prevail under the most adverse conditions as the slave of the black-guards Skull and Thomas Penn.

"You've been too long in the mountains, son," Lyman chided. "We've camped aplenty on the plains so far. You're thinking of being stuck here several days. A camp's more comfortable in the trees and high places where there's ample water and game, I'll grant you, but there are ways and special tricks for living out here, too. You'll see." Lyman grinned at Daniel.

Rachel spoke up. "We've more to do here than just take up space, Jake. Those two men caring for the sick are over-burdened."

"It's all worked out with Dr. Whitman, Rachel," he assured her. "We'll keep them in fresh meat."

"That simply is not enough, Jacob Lyman." When she called him by his full name, Jake knew it was her sweet way of chiding or scolding him, and he loved her for it.

"Do I take it Rachel that you've developed some plan?" He regarded her with a sly grin; he knew she had.

"I thought about it while you were down there making chin music with your Dr. Whitman."

Lyman sneaked a look at Daniel; the young man had half a smile at his mother's colorful word choice.

"All right," Lyman said, grinning openly at Rachel. "I'm ready for it."

"Minister for marrying or not, I planned on our staying here through their emergency."

"To do what, mother?" Daniel asked.

She looked at him and then back at Jake. "You two men amaze me sometimes with your ignorance. Or lack of imagination. The sick men down there will pass the crisis and get well and no longer be contagious. But they'll be frail for days. They'll be in the road to recovery and annoying Mr. Fontenelle and Dr. Whitman, who need to devote their energies to those still desperately ill."

"We could set up a what?. . .a recuperation camp!" Lyman caught her inspiration. Already he had developed a feeling of friendship toward the affable Mark Whitman. He looked forward to the ride back west; Whitman was a greenhorn, he thought, but an agreeable pilgrim who'd need plenty of wisdom in the ways of the woods to survive and adjust to—to enjoy and appreciate—his new and massively foreign surroundings. The West was as much different from Whitman's settled East as the surface of the moon. Lyman knew he could provide a needed element in that part of Dr. Whitman's education.

What Rachel had in mind would relieve Mark and Lucien as well as hasten the day he could arrange their marriage before Rev. Samuel Parker. And, as Rachel reminded him, get started back home; to their beloved Shinin' Mountains.

Rachel's voice invaded his thoughts. "Dr. Whitman could tell us what food supplies are in the wagons. There'd be little risk in contagion from them, especially after they were cooked. Fresh meat would bring strength to everyone."

"Could I take care of that, Jacob?" Daniel asked eagerly.

"Hunting? Maybe we both could, son. Or better, I'll ride guard for you while you get the meat. You've had experience, but I'd like to be with you."

The young man's expression glowed. "How soon can we start?"

Lyman looked at Rachel whose face radiated a mother's pride in a child developing into a responsible young man.

"We'd ought to set up our camp first for tonight," Lyman said. "Before, though, it'd be proper for me to call on the Reverend Mr. Parker. No point in fixing a recovery camp for the men until I talk with Dr. Whitman again. That ought to be first. It's yet mid-morning and these men will benefit from fresh meat as soon today as we can manage it. That's about the best answer I can give you, Daniel."

The young man was silent for a long moment. Clearly he was disappointed they couldn't start hunting immediately. His eyes were thoughtful. "Then what are we waiting for?" he said, almost whooping. "Let's get busy on our camp!"

Lyman gave Daniel—with his mother's approval and guidance—responsibility for selecting a site that would suit their needs both for their camp as well as a haven for convalescents, if Dr. Whitman agreed. Mother and son would begin to set up that camp while Jake went to call on Rev. Parker and again go down to speak with Dr. Whitman.

The preacher had left his book—a Bible—on his folding chair and had gone into his tent when Lyman strode up to it. "Reverend Parker?" he called.

"Who's that?" came the muffled response from inside the tent. A fifty-ish head poked out of the snow-white fly flaps. His expression was stern—Lyman harkened to Mark Whitman's word, "pragmatic"; Rev. Parker's expression said he would have little patience with almost any behavior that wasn't biblically proper.

"Lyman's the name, sir. Jacob Lyman. Rode in this morning."

Parker stepped out from the tent, his eyes surveying the man in well-worn, stained buckskins before him, clearly disapproving the coarse manner of his dress and by inference, his lifestyle.

"You know my name, Brother Lyman. You went below to chat with young Whitman. I suppose he spoke to you of my stubbornness in not wanting to become exposed further to the sins of the flesh of those dissolute blasphemers and frontier riffraff accompanying us."

Lyman sidestepped the minister's harsh words. "We spoke more of the critical nature of the sickness at the wagon camp."

"Mmm, I'm sure you did, Brother Lyman. Doctor Whitman and I are en route to the Oregon country to establish medical and ministerial missions to bring the word of God and Christian discipline to the heathen red man, Brother Lyman. At my age, I must take great care to avoid hazard that would hinder my commitment and my calling."

"I understand," Lyman said. "My family yonder plans to help Dr. Whitman and speed you on your way sooner."

"That'll be a blessing, Brother Lyman. What do you propose?"

"To move the convalescents away from the sickness when they're well enough recovered and aren't contagious. Rachel's son, the young man with us, will hunt for fresh meat for the camp. You'll be welcome to take meals with us, Reverend Parker, if Dr. Whitman approves our idea. I'm sure he will. I do have something to ask of you, though."

Reverend Parker appeared to dismiss Lyman's invitation and question by not responding. "If those heathen come under your care, Mr. Lyman, I'll have no truck with them, thank you anyway." Parker paused. "Your wife, Brother Lyman," he began, in an accusing, self-righteous tone. "From a distance she appears dark of skin and of straight black hair. Do you consort with a heathen squaw, Brother Lyman?"

Jake was taken aback by the abruptness and audacity of Parker's brazen question. He retained his composure.

"Rachel England is the widow of an army officer killed in the line of duty more than six years ago. As a result of the attack that claimed her husband, she was an Indian captive and separated from her son—also a captive—for five years before she successfully escaped."

Parker continued his prying and accusations, his tone and his questions irritating. "She must have been used for their foul needs. The young man with you appears to be blond, fair-skinned, resembling neither of you. Do we know its father?"

Lyman felt himself bristling with resentment of Rev. Parker for speaking ill of Daniel like some sort of sub-species creature. Or possibly a bastard. He kept his voice level.

"Reverend, with all due respect, I don't think these are issues that need concern you just now!"

Parker squinted suspiciously. "Do you hide something sinful yourself in the eyes of the Lord, Brother Lyman?"

Lyman found his patience sorely tried. "There are subjects of much greater concern here, Rev. Parker. Men may be dying down there and Mr. Fontenelle and Dr. Whitman desperately need assistance and relief. But in answer to your question, no, I have done nothing in my life to hide from any man."

"You speak of your family, but mention a Rachel England. Is she in fact Mrs. Lyman, and how long have you and she been one in the eyes of God?"

Lyman realized that in the eyes of this man from whom he had hoped to find cooperation, he had only snared himself in a semantic trap. "Things are different, much more difficult, on the frontier, Reverend."

"God's laws are universal! Self-denial, Lyman! Abstinence!"

"In our hearts we live as man and wife. Rachel was a widow five years when she escaped from Indian captivity. We found one another in the wilderness. We found love in our common need for survival."

"And copulated?"

Lyman knew he was too honest to be untruthful and could never leave a subject unfinished that created a false impression about him. Still he found despicable such prying into his private affairs. He had been taught at his grandmother's knee that men of the cloth commanded one's respect; without equivocation. And he had come to ask the minister to officiate at the wedding of him and Rachel—a precious, hallowed moment for both of them.

He responded with all the restraint at his command.

"If that is the way you choose to view it, Reverend Parker, yes, we have lived as husband and wife. A state of pure and true love and devotion. Anything that happened in her five years among the Indians was against her will, and without bearing on my feelings of love and dedication. Only now we travel to find proper authority to sanctify—"

"Concubinage, Brother Lyman, concubinage!" Parker's words were projected nasally and loudly as if from the pulpit. "It matters not if it is one or three-hundred. It is one and the same in principle and before the eyes of the Lord! It is evil if not sinful."

Lyman thought he had a valid counter-argument. "The Ten Commandments speak only against coveting and of adultery. I have committed neither sin!"

Parker's voice grew thick with exhortation. "And Solomon—with his three-hundred concubines—did evil in the sight of the Lord, as did David his father."

Lyman, finding himself clearly outmanned and outgunned, had had enough. "I'm sorry, Parson. I came to you hoping to find understanding and compassion. Instead, I am, in that fine old Scriptural sense, reviled. With all due respect, sir, I don't need you!" Lyman angrily spun on his heel and strode away leaving the bleached-haired old man standing, also livid in fury, beside his white canvas walled tent.

"Blessed is the man," Parker shouted after Lyman, his voice quivering at a high pitch to reach the ears of the man marching angrily away from him, "that walketh not in the counsel of the ungodly, nor standeth in the way of sinners, nor sitteth in the seat of the scornful!"

Rachel sensed Jake's fury as she watched his angry stride up the hill through dried, brittle grass from the tent of the aging man of God standing stiffly beside his solitary chair.

"It didn't go well?" she asked as he approached. Daniel was away some distance unloading a pack horse.

"Pious bastard!" Lyman muttered. "Forgive me, Rachel,

but the Reverend Samuel Parker, as Mark Whitman warned me, is a bumptious ass!"

"It did not go well." Now her words acknowledged the truth.

"Go tell Daniel not to unburden the pack horses. We'll ride on. Yet today. We can make many miles. To hell with Mark Whitman and Lucien Fontenelle! Let those men die as far as I'm concerned."

"Jacob Lyman! You can't mean that!"

"I mean just that! We'll never be married by that Testament-thumping thimblerigger! Here we are, ready to risk our very lives to bring comfort to the sick and dying and to a pair of saints putting their lives in jeopardy for their sakes and there stands that unctious coward finding scriptural reproach and justification for anything and everything the way he chooses to see it and judge it!"

"Jacob Lyman! Bite your tongue! Your anger only dignifies and stoops to the same level of hypocrisy as you say comes out of the mouth of Reverend Parker."

"Rachel, I'll not take from any man what he heaped on me! His own precious scriptures declare, 'judge not that ye be not judged.' He spoke of our love as concubinage and quoted Old Testament scripture to condemn it as evil and thus sinful."

Rachel looked off to where Daniel worried at the knots holding hitches on the pack animals; he was well beyond earshot.

"Jacob, I believe in the virtues of my upbringing. But if the past year and more with you has been sinful, then may I roast in hell!" Lyman caught a mischievous sparkle in the eyes of the woman he loved. Still the bitterness inside him was sour as bile.

Rachel edged closer to him. "Much as I yearned for Daniel over those tragic years and then your hopeful year of finding and bringing him to me, he has been an obstacle to the open expression of our love we had that winter in the old cabin. Then it was a burning question if he was even yet alive, and I fought my way back—with your precious help, Jacob Lyman—from five years of Indian captivity and the tragic loss of my beloved Edwin."

Close to her, Lyman acknowledged Rachel with his eyes, his seething fury against Samuel Parker softening in his closeness with the woman he loved.

Rachel grasped his arm. "Jacob Lyman, I will say this once. With all due respect to the theology and propriety of the Rev. Mr. Parker and the memory of Lieutenant Edwin England, you, Jacob Lyman, in this year of 1835, are my husband and may the devil take the hindmost if that is evil and sinful! If our love is never sanctified on the altar of God, He has blessed it on the altar of my heart."

Rachel's words had the effect of further calming Lyman's angry passions, and endearing him more deeply still to her.

"You're right, " he said. "Much as I've come to love Daniel and worked on him to become stronger after what he went through with those scoundrels, Skull and Thomas Penn, I miss those free, wonderful hours and days we shared that first winter at the cabin. The grizzly robe before our magical hearth. And we two alone. I suppose I haven't told you, Rachel, but those moments sustained me through a good many perilous times that followed before I was able to bring Daniel home to you."

"Daniel is eighteen. He's hardly re-entered my life but that I want him to get on with his. We need our times together again, Jacob."

Lyman felt himself totally at ease, his heart cleansed of its outrage as it filled with love—and sudden yearning—for the woman at his side. Though both of them loved him, Daniel's presence complicated their lives on many levels.

Lyman looked for Daniel at the pack horses, who stood unburdened and hobbled, nibbling at stalks of winter-cured yellow grass. Daniel had wandered away.

From behind him, Lyman heard a faint, pleading call and turned his intense concentration and closeness to Rachel to see the aging Rev. Samuel Parker making his hobbling way up the hill to where they stood amid their half-organized camp.

"Brother Lyman," Parker's frail voice entreated from the distance, "the cramps and the fever . . . I need your help. The scourge is upon me." He stumbled, began to fall, and Lyman raced to catch him.

Chapter Three

"WHERE'S MOTHER?" DANIEL STRODE UP, LEADING HIS HORSE, to find Jake sorting their gear before rigging their quarters under the shelter of the sky. As he paused, watching his lanky foster son's approach, Lyman's seasoned eye also roved his surroundings for a likely spot to care for Whitman's convalescents.

Against Jake's better judgment, Rachel had gone down-slope to look after the latest victim, and was at Rev. Parker's bedside in the virtually new white wall tent. Her insistence caused Lyman to grit his teeth and hold his tongue. In his unforgiving eyes, the pompous ass deserved no better than to die stewing in his own broth.

On edge over Rachel's exposure to the plague and con-cerned for her during the demanding days ahead, Lyman faced the errant Daniel in a low mood. "The question ought to go the other way, Daniel. Where've you been?" Jake heard the edge of impatience in his voice but, knowing Daniel wasn't the cause, took care not to unburden himself on the eager young man.

"Scouting, Jacob," Daniel said. "Not meant to trouble you. Thought I'd have a look-see. Where you and I'd find game when we get to meat hunting. Didn't go far. If I'd've seen hostiles—and you can be sure I would've if they'd been there—I'd've been in camp here long before they got an arrow notched in their bowstrings."

Lyman's mild flare of impatience at the boy's absence was quenched. In its place like a deep refreshing breath came a swell of pride. Some things, he thought, at least had a bright side. "You talk like a wintered-over hivernant, hoss! A right proper mountain man!" Lyman chuckled with the relief of some of his tension. Still he persisted in mock anger. "But, next time you decide to go out scouting on your own, pilgrim, you come and report to me first. If you get into an Indian fracas, I won't stand for you hoggin' all the glory when they show you their rumps and their heels."

Daniel beamed, understanding. "All right, Jacob." He hesitated, about to say more, but Lyman intruded, anxious about the work at hand.

"Just now though, young feller, there's something a good deal less glorious to face. That's laying our camp, tending to your mother's comforts, and looking to the security and browse for our riding and packing stock. I'm going to need help putting up a shade arbor handy to our camp for the comfort of those that survive the sickness yonder."

Lyman suddenly remembered another forgotten duty. "And somebody'd ought to take charge of Mr. Fontenelle's horses and mules yonder in the wagon circle. A man good with horses would take a few of them at a time to water and guard 'em while they graze. Between looking after all that and helping me rig things up here and then getting out to hunt a little, you could be pretty busy the next few days. Mr. Fontenelle and Dr. Whitman will sure be obliged if you'd look to their corralled stock."

Daniel dropped the reins to ground-tie his mount, his face flushed and his expression eager. "I'll start up here with our horses, Jacob. There's a creek yonder past that ridge. Runs over to the big river."

"Missouri," Lyman said.

"Yes, sir," Daniel acknowledged, coming closer to break the silence with something he wanted to say moments before like an afterthought. "Jacob, if there'd've been hostiles out there in all those hills of grass now, you can bet I'd've seen 'em," he repeated. "You forget I lived among 'em, the fine ones and the evil ones. I pretty much know how they think and what they'll do. I sometimes wish you wouldn't worry about me so much—you and mother. Then I remember how long it was *nobody* cared much whether I lived or died, and I get kind of. . .well, I'm *grateful!*" So far, since his return, Daniel had difficulty—hemmed and hawed—when it came to expressing how he felt.

Warmed by the young man's revelation, Lyman was also aware that it had come from somewhere buried deep.

"I'm proud of you for being man enough to say those things, Daniel. Pleased to know your feelings and pleased you're having them." His own words sounded stiff and awkward as they spilled off his lips, especially after the depth of Daniel's disclosures.

Daniel was thoughtful a moment before grabbing a big breath. These moments of closeness—and openness—especially with Lyman, were still foreign to him, too. "Guess I'd best water our mounts and hobble 'em in the grass. Then I'll get busy with Mister Fontenelle's stock. I'll help you rig the camp for the sick people, too, when you need me, Jacob. How does that sound?"

Lyman, reluctant now to drop the trend of their talk, evaded Daniel's question for the moment. "Agreeable . . . son, we've not spoken much of those evil years yet, have we?"

A distant look came into the young man's eyes, his thoughts spinning back to the terrible, wasted times. He spoke softly, almost hoarse with emotion. "No, sir."

"When your mother and I are properly husband and wife in God's eyes and get back home, you and I can go somewhere and make a hunting camp. Give us a chance for a long palaver."

Daniel studied Jake, his features knotted over coming to grips with what was troubling him. "I'd like it if maybe we could get to it sooner, Jacob. Mother asks me so often about it. She . . . persists. I don't ever want to hurt her, but I don't know how to tell her either! So much wouldn't be good for her to know. That's why it's hard for me to speak with her. To know what and what not to say. I feel like an ungrateful son in not being honest or that I'm being . . ." Daniel paused, searching for the right words.

"Evasive?" Lyman prompted. In the months since Lyman rescued him from his evil captivity, the boy's memory of his native language had come back strongly. Certain words and phrases, Lyman was aware, were still tucked away yet to come out, if they'd ever been there at all. But, Lyman also thought, the lad caught on quickly.

"Maybe that's the word, Jacob. You could help me find other words, gentle words to use to tell her about it. You knew Thomas Penn and you knew Skull and how they used me. Tried to make me a worthless killer and their camp slave. You know very little of the years before; the way I was treated among the Indians. I need to find the words to tell mother, but spare her the awful parts—the sinful parts."

Lyman reached across and affectionately gripped Daniel's shoulders with his hands for reassurance, feeling his eyes going misty. "Remember this, boy. Rachel's a strong woman," he said, using her first name with her son for the first time. "She lived through much of the same agony of Indian captivity. But you're right," Jake agreed. "We shouldn't wait. The sooner we talk, the better. Now, of course, isn't the time. Things'll smooth out in a day or so. We'll have to get out together and hunt. I'll watch for the opportunity and make it seem natural. To her. I'll help you all I can. Meanwhile, there's work to be done here."

"I'll get busy with the horses."

"Right enough," Lyman responded. "It won't take three shakes for me to lay our place up here, and line out 'Camp Recovery.' Quick as I get that done, I must get back down to Dr. Whitman, tell him what we have in mind."

Daniel strode away with a meaningful "Thank you, Jacob." Mulling over the significance of his foster son's welcome adjustment to his sometimes bewildering new life, Lyman turned to setting up camp, trampling down and pulling up the tinder-like grass near their place of buffalo-chip fires for cooking and night warmth and deciding on placement of the convalescents' bedding ground. Daniel would be some time watering and securing their horses in a good area for grazing, as well as caring for Fontenelle's stock.

Before going down to talk again with Marcus Whitman, Jake thought of looking in on Rachel and her care of the ailing Rev. Parker. "No," he thought, "let the stiff-necked old goose draw his own conclusions about this Jezebel headed for perdition and hell's eternal damnation. Or let him die!"

Rachel's gentle, caring ways, Lyman thought, would change the obstinate old cross-grain's opinions of her wicked ways.

He shushed himself as a fool for sputtering in his head about Parker. Rather, he thought, Marcus Whitman and Lucien Fontenelle deserved his attention. He took advantage of the lull to make his way back down to the wagon camp and signal Marcus Whitman. Again they met at a safe, respectable distance from Whitman's hasty treatment area where men writhed in their blankets in pain, or lay spiritless as corpses, their vitality sapped by illness.

"Reverend Parker's fallen victim, Mark," Lyman said as he walked up. "Got halfway up to where we propose to camp before he about fell over. I caught him. Rachel's with him now, caring for him. He spoke of stomach cramps and fever, Mark," Lyman explained. "And, sad to say, we've both now been exposed."

"He walked up to your camp, you say, Jake?"

"Part way, almost there before he near collapsed."

"Not the symptoms I've seen here. When it hits, a man can't so much as move. Best described as 'deathly ill.' Reverend Parker may have a mild attack. But there really is no such thing with cholera. I'll look in on him directly."

Lyman weighed the idea of telling Whitman of his troubling conversation with Rev. Parker, but thought better of it. Marcus Whitman had enough on his mind. Lyman decided to stick to brighter subjects.

"We've an idea how we can help you down here, Mark. I've even started. A convalescent camp, you might say, up the hill there, close to us. For those out of danger and not contagious. Take a load off you and Lucien. The three of us can look after them in fine fashion, get some good food into them. Speed their recovery. Our young man, Daniel, is to look after Lucien's stock in the wagon compound."

Whitman's face came alive with relief. "The Lord surely works in wondrous ways! That's a capital idea, Jake! There are one or two ready to go now. They need to get away from the sickness and rebuild their strength. You give me the perfect answer. And so much hope. God surely sent you and your family."

"Oh, just passin' through, Mark. We're not the kind to turn our backs on folks in need."

"You and your lady have good hearts. Maybe Reverend Parker's ailments won't affect you and Rachel. Some it gets to; others it doesn't. But, I'd begun to wonder if I'd discover decency in the West. And a gracious Lord saw fit to deliver to me you and your Rachel."

Whitman's expression tightened. "They've not been the most charitable or hospitable since we asked to join them in St. Louis, Jake. That crowd I tend over yonder. Lucien's openly showed his resentment, figuring the two of us more a nuisance than anything. He's at the jug as much or more than they are. It's difficult. All my life, I've opposed the use of spirits."

"Sorry to say, and sad for you, but Lucien's pretty well known for that," Lyman said softly.

"The workmen were openly rude and he did nothing to control them. They even tried to discourage and drive away Reverend Parker and me by pelting us with rotten eggs, and taunting us with other despicable behavior."

Lyman grunted in disgust, but Whitman grinned. "Reverend Parker turned away from them in anger, but I determined not to be spiteful. I did my best to meet their unkindness with Christian tolerance. I hardly view this cholera outbreak as divine providence, but it surely has turned the tables. All of a sudden, nearly every one of those men is glad that a medical doctor is on hand and is grateful for my care. I haven't cured their miseries. Only time can do that. But I've saved lives and found ways, and with herbs and medications, to ease their suffering."

Whitman crossed his arms over his chest and looked wistfully back at the sprawling rows of ailing men. "Not altogether successful, Jake. I haven't told you. I've lost two and another won't survive. The dead need proper burial. Doesn't inspire those ailing to always be reminded of the dead nearby."

"Sorry to hear that, Mark," Lyman responded. "Soon's I get things organized up yonder for the walking wounded, I'll get busy on a burial detail. My stepson, Daniel, will be around to help. I plan to build a big shade arbor for them to rest under as they recuperate."

"Could have used something like that down here."

"It'd take some time, but I could build one down here, too."

"Ah, Jake, you've already taken on enough. God bless you . . . and your family. You know, you and I make quite a team," Whitman said, grinning despite his burden of fatigue. "Whitman and Lyman. It has a good sound."

"I'm honored," Jake said.

"Not near so much as I, Jacob. I'll tell Lucien of your plans."

Trudging back uphill, Lyman studied the gently rolling hills of grass—the "flatlands" despised by trappers—nearby where the Platte met the Missouri; they'd come out of the Shinin' Mountains following the South Platte bound east to find a minister to take the first necessary, formal step to make them a family.

There was nothing wrong with flatlands, Lyman mused, looking around him, but that they lacked in inspiration, or maybe challenge; monotonous was the word. Mountains offered a new feast for the eyes beyond every ridge, around every boulder that blocked a man's vision.

And trees. Flatland trees—what there were of them, which was few—didn't have to put up much of a fight of it. Except maybe against the wind which seemed an almost constant companion out here. Then, they simply bent with it and were warped or stunted in their growth. Still, flatland soil was rich and deep, water near the surface. Around here a tree could plunge its roots as deep and as free as it cared to.

But, Lord, the trees on the mountains, he thought. To stand tall up there, the tangy-smelling green pines and the fir built hefty muscle and knot-hard calluses and scars to climb over rocks searching a place to grip in a crack, anything to hold onto and reach down. Even when a tree rooted in surface soil up there, the unyielding bedrock lurked, not that much below the surface to challenge the striving for life.

Maybe, Lyman thought, just maybe there was the answer; this striving for life. Perhaps there truly was a difference between mountaineers and flatlanders. The plainsman must have it easier; the soil was softer, more beckoning.

Loam and coarse granite gravel had little in common.

Like a mountain pine, fir or spruce, hemlock or cedar, a mountain man—if he was to survive—had to dig in with fingers and toes and sometimes teeth, just to hang on and suck a meager existence out of thin, gravelly soil.

And, no matter how hard you tried, the mountains were unforgiving. Your roots could go deep and your crown of branches stand tall against the sky. You could think yourself invincible; that you could take on all comers. Even then the elements could wither you—challenge your grip—and the first good wind could send you crashing down never to rise again, to decay in the very soil that nourished you.

But in that challenge stout-hearted men were bred; Jake Lyman considered himself one of them.

Suddenly he yearned to get home; to be back there.

But delaying here to assist Marcus Whitman, Lyman thought, was a task worthy of the challenge. The only preacher with the authority they had come all this way to find, was bull-headed and hypocritical; Lyman doubted that after his bitter confrontation with Rev. Parker that the man would even consider performing the ceremony to unite him and Rachel.

He shook his head, feeling his spirits sinking; they might have to continue on, all the way to St. Louis, a place he had forsaken years before. He hated the prospect of returning. "Jake!" Rachel's voice intruded on his thoughts from behind him. Brightness drove away the dark cloud of his thinking as he turned to see his beloved wife—wife at least in his eyes and in his heart—trudging happily toward him on an angle from Rev. Parker's white-canvas tent. She hurried her steps to join him on his trek up the hillside of grass.

"How is your patient?" Lyman let her catch up with him and, oblivious to contagion, threw his arm around her shoulders joyfully as together they climbed the hill toward their campsite in carefree, affectionate embrace.

Rachel's face was bright and flushed with pleasure. "He'll live, Jake. Magnified his symptoms, I'm afraid. Surely he doesn't have the ailment those down there do. I think Rev. Parker caught a slight cold. A touch of an upset stomach from something he ate went along with it. He's resting. His uproar with you may have dispirited him, too. I think more than anything else, he was lonely. I learned as a little girl that the self-righteous do tend to be withdrawn and lonely. But, we had a nice long talk. He's grateful and was moved that I'd risk the dangers to care for him."

"People can't stay out of sorts long around you, Rachel."

Her eyes beamed on his as they walked.

"I told him about us, of my losing Edwin so tragically, and the captivity and how you tried so hard to find Daniel for almost a year. His attitude has changed, Jake. He understands us now and doesn't find so much of our being together so troubling."

"And?"

"And he's eager and excited about performing a ceremony for us!"

Chapter Four

ON A DAY THAT SEEMED TO THE BRIDEGROOM BRIGHTER AND sunnier than any in his recollection, Jake stood stiff but glowing and expectant, Rachel at his side, in the shade of the same arbor where most of the throng of smiling but still haggard witnesses—today, all obligingly sober—spent their days of recuperation.

For the most part crude and loud braggarts, brawlers, and heavy drinkers, Fontenelle's now meek *engagees* had come to close grips with the deadly cholera and survived, thanks in large measure to the talented and tireless Dr. Marcus Whitman. Their leader, often deeper into the jug than most of them, had had a closer call with death from cholera than Lyman realized.

The *engagees* also knew and had grown close to the Lymans—as they were known—especially the gentle ministering angel they found in Rachel during their days of pleasant convalescence under the ample shade arbor. There they had rested, talked, and were well-fed and cared for as they regained their strength.

Lyman, beaming at them as he awaited his wedding ceremony, saw new friends, men who had come up the hill as emaciated skeletons barely alive and now, a week and a half later, were well on the road to full recovery. Their wasted, gleaming but grateful eyes were mostly on the woman beside him; Rachel, with her caring, giving, gentle ways, had won their hearts. To them, she deserved sainthood.

On his other side, still in his nearly unsmudged buck-skins—the man most responsible for saving the crew from total catastrophe—Dr. Marcus Whitman beamed his pride in his role as Jake's best man. Next to Rachel in a new colorful and blousy calico shirt and wool breeches bought at a trading post in anticipation of the occasion, stood a polished and well-groomed Daniel England representing, more or less, the traditional approval of Rachel's family to the ceremony.

As if in honor of the occasion as well, in the vast sweep of slow-rolling country on all sides of the arbor, the sun out of a clear sky of azure-blue turned the cured grass to gleaming gold. A furtive groundwind flirted delicately across it giving it life like the surface of a gentle sea. Pairs of small white butterflies flitted randomly a few feet above the sun-warmed grass. The air, too, in Jake Lyman's mellowed senses, had a warm and festive gaiety all its own. From somewhere, not far, a lark trilled a happy anthem to his wedding day.

Trembling but feeling his prime and the fullness of joy in his chest, Lyman watching the aging Rev. Parker toil formally uphill from his tent, his black suit proudly brushed and unwrinkled, a low and flat-crowned black hat with a wide, flat brim fitted straight and shoved down close to his ears. For the occasion, Rev. Parker affected a stock at his throat, a wide and stiff white cloth cravat out of style any more except now and then among older clergymen. It was no doubt carefully preserved most of the time in a box or wallet among Parker's ministerial trappings in his possibles.

The preacher from New York State hugged his large black Bible under one arm, the fingers of his other hand marking two places. His bearing seemed stern as he continued his uphill stride toward the arbor. As he neared the congregation, Lyman saw with a spurt of delight the minister's smile, though hardly a broad one, and his eyes sparkled, something Jake certainly hadn't seen in his first encounter with the testy Oregon-bound missionary. A respectful human aisleway opened down the center of the long, shady rectangle on the prairie hillside; Rev. Parker's bearing, his ministerial presence, and his pace from the arbor's far end lent an air of reverence to the occasion.

As Parker passed Lucien Fontenelle standing at the head of his crew, close to the wedding party, the rangy, craggy-faced caravan leader spoke up: "Mornin', Parson."

Parker's head flicked at Fontenelle, his brows dropped to hood his now-sparking eyes at the rude intrusion into the solemnity he had created in this moment. Cowed by the fierce scowl and put in his place by it, Fontenelle's shoulders slumped, his features working in an embarrassed, sheepish grimace.

Parker swung around to come nearly face to face with Jake and Rachel watching him apprehensively. Parker's degree of restraint among Fontenelle's workmen was fragile and just now Lyman knew he, himself, would be intolerant of any threat to these wonderful moments and for the sake of the woman he loved at his side. Rev. Parker's face brightened as he turned to them and abruptly it became frozen again as he spun back to face the assembled American Fur Company workmen and their leader.

"Dammit!" Lyman thought. "Here it comes. He's going to have something to say about their behavior." He reached down and caught Rachel's hand and squeezed it anxiously; she squeezed back in recognition and understanding of his fears.

In the comfort of her warm, soft hand in his, Lyman tensed himself against sudden reaction to whatever Parker would have to say.

"Brethren," the preacher began in a surprisingly gentle tone, "three weeks ago we came into this valley of the shadow of death where many of us were tested most severely with evil affliction. Perhaps as God's way of showing the survivors the wages of straying from paths of righteousness, three of us will rest for eternity in these hills. Now, as we prepare to witness and celebrate the joyous occasion of joining forever the hands and lives of two of our company, let us observe a moment of silent prayer for those departed who sleep in yonder graves. As we do, let us thank God for our deliverance from the serpent's sting. And in that spirit of thanksgiving, let us each in his own way ponder the course of his life and highly resolve to conduct himself closer to the embrace of the great, everlasting arms of a loving and merciful God."

As Rev. Parker's head bowed, his hand came up to shield his closed, prayerful eyes while the other, fingers still marking their places, clutched his Bible at his side. Before he closed his eyes, Lyman noted with grim satisfaction that Fontenelle's crewmen all stood with reverently bowed heads.

With his other arm, Jake lightly nudged Mark Whitman in acknowledgement and thanks. Without Whitman, Lyman realized, these moments might never have come. In friendly fashion, Whitman's elbow levered out to nudge Lyman back. Jake turned his head and opened his eyes to see a broad, amiable grin on Whitman's face, and his joy swelled even fuller at their growing camaraderie.

In a few moments, Rev. Parker cleared his throat more for attention than anything and murmured a loud "ah-men." The response from those of Fontenelle's crew who had ever been to church, was mostly a broad "a-men." Nearly two dozen bright faces still seamed with the strain of illness, came alert to the quartet facing them from the end of the arbor as Rev. Parker turned back to Jake and Rachel, his expression calm and benevolent. He flipped the Bible open to one of his marked passages and held it before him as his eyes darted back and forth between those of Jake and Rachel.

"Dearly beloved," be began, his eyes searching theirs deep with meaning, "we are gathered together in the sight of God and in the presence of this company on this glorious hallelujah day to join this man and this woman in the bonds of holy matrimony . . ."

* * *

AS THEIR TRAIL traced the serpentine Platte River westward, upriver, it was only after days of toiling across monotonous, slow-rolling prairieland that their surroundings even began to develop into what might be charitably called rugged terrain.

The thick green of lush-leafed trees skirted the river and here and there dotted the land in woodlots or as scattered and solitary dots of shade in vast sunlit fields. They were nothing, in Lyman's seasoned eye, to his ancestors' once-proud eastern woodlands nor the legions of mighty needled monarchs that silently flowed across his beloved Shinin' Mountains.

"They're starting to call it the Great Plains," Jake explained to Marcus Whitman as the two of them rode well in advance of Fontenelle's caravan of trade goods from St. Louis. Lucien pushed the train as fast as his flagging stamina and that of his weakened men would allow; the three-week halt by the epidemic had eaten valuable time; Fontenelle was impatient to get his cargo of trade goods to rendezvous at New Fork on the Green River.

To help—as the Lymans made their way back west—the newlywed Jake and Rachel and Daniel England became temporary *engagees* of the American Fur Company. In a wagon more lightly loaded with food supplies and cooking gear, with one of the strongest teams under the skilled hands of a good driver, Rachel forged ahead to find likely places for the noon stop and to get a hot, bracing meal ready for men not yet quite up to the demands of the trail or the need for speed and long hours. After the noon cleanup and packing supplies and utensils, Rachel and her assistant rolled past the caravan to seek a likely site along the river for the travelers' night camp.

Her operation was smooth, the men content and grateful and less dependent on whiskey; Fontenelle, despite his own fondness for the jug and his anxieties about time to be made up, was pleased with their progress. Hardly complacent, Lucien still hurried his wagon drivers along.

Daily, Lyman and Daniel scouted protectively a short distance ahead of Rachel's wagon, separated on the flanks of their trail, alert to hostile activity as well as for fresh meat for Rachel's pots—Fontenelle's *engagees* had ravenous appetites.

Lyman was pleased when Dr. Whitman, who spent a great deal of his time with Rev. Parker and shared the wall tent at night with the missionary, varied his daily routine with several hours of riding the Platte River grasslands alongside Jake. He imagined that Whitman's long hours with the Rev. Parker would become anything other than tedious.

"For a long time," Jake continued, surveying the limitless easy country and lush grass in all directions, "they called all this the Great American Desert. Now they see greater promise in farming and grazing out here with the frontier pushing farther west, and find a more hospitable name for it."

"I'm anxious to get to the mountains, Jake. Determine what it'll take to cross them into Oregon. To find out if wagons can get through. We'll need to haul in freight for our missions. A lot of it!"

"Not been tried that I know of. That's not to say it's not possible. Lucien's taking us west up the North Platte. Along here, it's just called the Platte. We'll be past the mouth of the South Platte soon, Mark, where what's known as the North Platte commences to bear west by north."

"Lucien's driving himself to the limit. Seems to think his strength can come out of the bottle. To me that's like whipping a jaded horse, Jake. Has he spoken to you of his plans?"

"None but that we follow the North Platte to Fort Laramie. Where his business partner Tom Fitzpatrick's waiting."

"Last night in a more sober moment, he told me that when he gets the caravan to the fort, he plans to drop off and stay there and recuperate and let somebody named

Broken Hand take the caravan on to rendezvous. He's a beaten man, Jake. Not just physically. He's dispirited."

"I've noticed. The man you speak of *is* Fitzpatrick. Some Indians call him Bad Hand. Old injury of some sort. Got stiff fingers on one hand. But let me tell you he's not crippled. They don't come any stouter than Tom Fitzpatrick."

"I thought with that name, he might be an Indian. I'm told they often have peculiar names . . . by our standards, I mean."

Lyman grinned. "So do mountain men, Mark. In some circles, I'm known as Griz Killer."

"I suppose there's a story behind that, too."

"Not much, Mark. I'll tell you some time. Mountaineers turn simple happenings into wondrous legend around a campfire."

"Some skeptics say that about the Scriptures."

"I wouldn't know," Lyman said dryly. "Lucien's looked a little peaked to me since we left the Missouri and the time of his sickness. Actin' strange, I'll say that. And his way with the bottle worries me. As I asked, he stayed off whiskey and was good-natured for my wedding. I'm grateful for that. Since then, Lucien seems have burrowed inside himself and doesn't often come out. Be that as it may, Tom Fitzpatrick knows the way to this season's rendezvous like the back of his hand, broken or otherwise."

"Green River, Lucien told me. Is it really green, Jake?"

"Under other circumstances, Mark, that might come as a foolish question. But the river does have a greenish cast to it, as you'll see when we get there. And the land around it is green; rich with green. In trees," Lyman responded, chuckling, at ease with his newfound companion. A pilgrim, he thought. But a pilgrim with promise. Marcus Whitman would be good in—and good for—this land. Lyman's "shinin' times" in the Shinin' Mountains—in spite of his soul's close-guarded and jealous hold on his place in them and the wonders of their vastness—were changing.

More men coming in with the same kind of hunger for the unending sprawl of space to live and breathe and work and build and revel and love and fight and die. In spite of himself, Lyman knew, he had to step aside and make room— even for such as Mark Whitman. Room to paw and beller and stretch themselves to the limits of land and sky, awakened to a new day—and a new life.

"And sure enough green compared to here," he went on. "You'll see. That country. Inspirin', Mark. Trees, green year-round, thick as hog bristles except on those wondrous-tall rocky peaks. And maybe you'll come to love it as I do. A great deal depends on the man, Mark. You have to meet this country. On its terms. You don't fight it. Or try to bend it to your whims. You flow with its rhythms. It's green, Mark, and ever-fresh and new. And while it's hostile and deadly, it's also rugged and demanding to a man, but it's rich. Rich in potential and rich in future. I've changed now that I've shucked my bachelor ways; my sights are on wife and family. It was great for me to come of age in. Now it's great country for a man to build a family and a future for those who come after. To stand tall and proud and be responsible . . . to himself and to those around him. And responsible to the land—and his country—that nourishes them and gives them a decent, hopeful base for sinking their roots."

Lyman stopped, took off his hat and swiped a sleeve across a sweaty forehead, chuckling self-consciously. They paused to rest the horses in the sun-spread grassland. He caught a glimpse in the distance of Daniel riding the left flank, watching them curiously. From behind him, he heard the approaching rattle of Rachel's wagon.

"Listen to me, would you! I commence to sound like Reverend Parker preaching from the pulpit. Back to the here and now, Mark. Rendezvous is in striking distance of your Oregon country. Some north of the best route and still a good ways. New Fork is high up on Green River toward its source. If Fontenelle says Fitzpatrick's waiting at Fort

Laramie, he'll be best served to let Tom guide the caravan in. It's not easy, that last leg from Laramie—and sure won't be for a man as weakened as Lucien Fontenelle. At least it's well-marked, well-known and well-used. Up the Sweetwater over South Pass. Then from where the Sweetwater rises it's not more'n a hoot and a holler west to the Green."

He glanced at Whitman who rode beside him watching emerging distant bluffs to the west with a faraway look; his thoughts seemed as distant as the horizon.

"Something wrong, Mark?"

"What?" Whitman responded like a man coming awake. "Ah, no, Jake. The good times with you and Rachel and Daniel; your wedding . . ." He paused, studying Lyman, his face thoughtful.

"Is there someone back there, Mark? For you? Waiting?"

Whitman's eyes turned distant again. "Indeed. And she'll be with me—in this new land. To build a life together and to fulfill our covenant with God. Narcissa. Narcissa Prentiss. Darling, delightful woman . . . as committed to God's work as I am. She's been accepted by the American Board of Commissioners for Foreign Missions of the church.

"This year, Jake, I only go as far as rendezvous. Reverend Parker will go on to establish a base in Oregon. I'll go back and gird for the truly ambitious effort, a wagon caravan of our own with other missionary families to the Oregon country."

Lyman grunted.

"Does that surprise you, Jake?"

Now Lyman was the thoughtful one; someone once told him that nothing was so constant as change. "No. Seems like a long trip just to see how the land lies and then have to go back. But it's sound judgment. There's damned little information back east about this country and most of it's faulty if not downright irresponsible in ignoring the dangers. Bad information is worse than no information to a greenhorn."

"But I'll at least have one friend deep in this country— you, Jake. Perhaps after rendezvous, I'll have more. If they're unable to physically guide me, at least I'll have the benefit of wise counsel."

Lyman reflected a few moments before responding. Whitman's remark approached using a friendship freely given; he would not knowingly be used by anyone. But, his reasoning followed, Mark Whitman was not a devious, scheming man, but a pious and open one. Decisively, he threw his lot for good and all with the medical missionary from New York State.

"At rendezvous, Mark. you're going to see wild sights that may turn your eyes and your stomach, behavior you've not considered nor seen before. I think I know the kind of man you are. Understanding and caring. The 'doin's,' as we say, at rendezvous may try your patience. But beware of harsh judgments, my friend. This is the one time in the year that these men get to rare up and paw the air, to be with old friends. Whiskey—that you despise—is there in abundance. In a dimension beyond your ken and your craw will be dissipation, wild behavior, profanity, and Reverend Parker's dreaded word, 'concubinage.' It will be a trial of restraint for you, but I venture that you'll weather it better than Reverend Parker. He may retreat again as he did at Bellevue when the cholera hit. I think of a couple of men there who can be of great help to you—Jim Bridger and Joe Meek. Remember the names. I can't think of others more knowing of this land—in their love and their awe of it—than Bridger and Meek. Bridger the grim, but the great tale-spinner, and Meek, who in no way lives up to his name, but is the spreader of joy and lover of life and the carefree. Believe me, Mark, both will seem less on the surface than what lurks in the depths beneath. These are sincere, substantial men who know this land. Men who'll not resent being leaned upon if they trust you as an equal. But that's something that must be earned. I can't give it to you. Nor explain it. There is a mystery, a code—a covenant, if you will—in this country, too, Mark, that no man can buy his way into.

It must be earned. By dint of exposure and suffering. You must earn their trust as they learn to trust you."

Riding alongside him through the rolling grasslands of the upper Platte, Marcus Whitman was also thoughtful.

"Wise and wide counsel, Jacob. I'm in your debt."

"You owe me nothing, Dr. Whitman," Lyman declared. "Because of your influence, Rachel and I are one. I've only one last word on the subject and we'll get back to guiding Lucien's caravan on to Fort Laramie. Beware, Dr. Whitman, of what you represent in this land."

"I don't understand, Jake," Whitman interrupted. "I come as a healer, an apostle of the saving grace, of strength, and well-being."

"At New Forks, there may be resentment of you. Especially Reverend Parker and his ways, Mark. Open and aggressive resistance of what you stand for in their eyes. This is the challenge I spoke of before. Bridger and Meek, Joseph Walker, Tom Fitzpatrick, and men of kindred stamp are one thing. They're the leaders. Beware the underlings, Dr. Whitman. They're a powerful force to reckon with. This land is changing, Mark, and the mountaineers—the trappers—themselves are the least tolerant of change.

"They hold tight a vain pride that they were the ones who met the country on its terms and survived and made a living and built a life. They'll oppose new ideas, new approaches. Change—a destruction of their hard-earned way of life—is loathsome of them, Mark. If you thought that the pestering of Fontenelle's *engagees* was rude, I dread what you may encounter at rendezvous."

Chapter Five

WALKING FEATHER OF THE CROWS, WITH TWO CLATTERING horse-drawn travois, their poles sagging under heavy packs of his year's catch of prime beaver plews and a third with his lodge and belongings, brought his family down from the land to the north, bound for the white man's trading fair south of the headwaters of the Seeds-kee-dee.

The whites at Fort Van Buren where Walking Feather and the Crows traded at other times of the year spoke of the river named for the prairie hen now as "greenriver." The word sounded nothing like Seeds-kee-dee. White man's talk often confused Walking Feather; he tried hard to distinguish and identify white man's words and to use them, knowing he had more power over the traders when he could understand and speak their words. Men who did not know the white man's schemes and failed to learn some of his words were viciously cheated in trading and easily fell under the influence of the traders' vile whiskey and for it surrendered their hard-earned beaver pelts, their women, and their horses. And their dignity.

Even more confusing, the same white traders and trappers and river men swore by a simple wood-hafted, curved-blade sheath knife for skinning and butchering they also called "greenriver." Walking Feather had even traded for one and had come to depend on it. He often held and pondered his greenriver knife, trying to fathom the white man's words and his superior wisdom and ways. Nothing about the knife suggested a river or a prairie hen. Other words in the white man's tongue were equally bewildering.

Moving down the Seeds-kee-dee, the family of Walking Feather—his wife, Moon-That-Grows, best known as Moon, and his young daughters, Soft Wind and Grass Woman—controlled a herd of twelve fine plains mustangs that he had stolen from enemies (sometimes whites), captured wild, or traded from other Crow villages.

These he also brought to trade with the white merchants from the East or with the hairy faced mountain men in return for the essentials he and his women would need in the year ahead. He also wanted to get something special this year for each one of them. Almost more than his horses, Walking Feather was proud and protective of his wife and daughters.

Moon had suffered greatly with the birth of Grass Woman and her seed was no longer good. Walking Feather would die without a son. It had now been fifteen summers; this, he thought, was as it must be.

His daughters would marry strong warriors and make him many grandsons to be proud of. Viewing his situation this way, Walking Feather lavished his affection and his fathering on Soft Wind and her sister, a year younger, Grass Woman.

Walking Feather found himself both excited about the prospect of the trading and apprehensive of the time of the fur fair. Moon had not yet taken on all of the scars and seams and sags of age, and the hungry eyes of the river men and the hairy-faced trappers followed her when she went with Walking Feather to the river posts to trade. Soft Wind and Grass Woman had developed, too, since last year, their body parts pressing against soft buckskin dresses in places men found provocative. Their legs and arms were lithe and soft and brown, their moccasined steps tantalizing. Walking Feather pondered it all in dismay.

While trying to strike favorable bargains with the traders for his beaver and avoiding the temptation of whiskey that could addle his brain, Walking Feather knew he had to be on guard for the virtue of his women. At the fur fair, the white mountain men thronging the rendezvous grounds and often wild with drink, could be relentless and abusive of Indian women who shunned their advances. A man could be shot down dead for protecting the virtue of a daughter or a wife and few of the white trappers would care.

Walking Feather was troubled with what he had seen happen after the eager, fetching young women at rendezvous fell prey to the worthless geegaws, the whiskey and the insistent urgings of the hungry and heartless celebrating trappers. Too soon the soft and beautiful, nut-brown girls tumbled to the spell of the whiskey, dependent on it, selling themselves for a sip or a drop. And finally begging and crying. They aged too soon, became shrieking, sagging, worthless, and toothless old crones, withered before their time. They were no longer attractive to eager, young warriors for marriage, and too easily afflicted with the white man's burden in plagues of the coughs and of the crotch. Too soon their forgotten bones littered the plains like the slaughtered buffalo.

Walking Feather vowed to himself and on the sacred medicine bundles of his fathers that none of this would destroy Moon, nor Soft Wind nor Grass Woman.

Going down the Seeds-kee-dee with his women and his worldly belongings, Walking Feather met and traveled with three other Crow families, one of whom he knew. He noted with inward pride that none had as many travois' or horses as he, and none so loaded with beaver. Neither did any have wives and daughters as comely as Moon and Soft Wind and Grass Woman. One sleep before reaching the trappers' fair, they were joined by parties of friendly Bannacks and Shoshones who also had met on the trail and traveled together.

Their caravan soon amounted to twelve families with horse herds and riding mounts and those dragging travois', the women chattering as they rode or walked along, children frolicking and laughing, and dogs foraging or snapping at each other, the mass of people and animals random in formation and stretching back for nearly a mile.

Walking Feather was certain their dust cloud would be seen from rendezvous well ahead of their arrival. He heard them before he saw them beyond a sloping ridge they toiled up to approach the wide valley the white man called New Fork. A muted murmur of sound lifted up from the basin ahead like soft rain returning to the sky. Peppery rifle shots barked through the sound with the snap of frozen limbs in the dark night stillness of the Moon of Popping Trees.

Riding well ahead of the caravan with his Crow friend and a head man from a Shoshone village, Walking Feather crested the ridge to look down on the churning mass of white men and Indians that resembled nothing more than the tiny white wiggle-worms when they infest putrid flesh.

"Many men," the Crow, Standing Dog, remarked. He was a gentle man with a mean face.

"But not so many as last time," the Shoshone observed dryly, his glinting eye taking in the scene below them. "This may not be a good time for trade."

Walking Feather was puzzled. "Why would it not be?"

"Only one place for trading," the Shoshone answered. He had never given Walking Feather his name. "See? At their place, I do not see many wagons of the things to trade. They have only one fur press. In the years before, there were many wagons and many fur presses. Maybe the white man is finished here and will leave this country. My people will rejoice."

"I see now," Walking Feather said. "The trading tables and the fur presses and the many wagons of Fontenelle and *Casapy*, "Blanket Chief" Bridger and Bad Hand are gone this year. This disturbs me. Not enough trade goods to go around so they will demand even more of plews in trade."

"We are days behind in getting here," Standing Dog said. "Everyone else is already here, and their trading is done. We must hurry our people and have our women unpack the travois' and raise the lodges that we may trade before everything is gone."

"We are not that late," Walking Feather argued. "I see several lodges with the poles in place but with coverings not yet raised. These people are only just here. The grass is hardly yet disturbed by people and horses. It is early yet. It must be that Fontenelle, *Casapy* Bridger, and Bad Hand are late this year. We will ride in and they will tell us."

Urging their horses downslope, they entered the welter of huge cone-shaped lodges and white trappers and Indians trudging about or clustered around fires talking and laughing. At one end of the camp, shooters-at-the-mark vied for prizes or a cash pot put up by the contestants.

From a distance, away off in the sprawling basin, Walking Feather could see crowds of men watching as two riders raced their horses for prizes and for wagering opportunities for those in the crowd.

Out of the excitement and hectic activity around him, Walking Feather sensed his blood racing in anticipation; through all of the year, most of his days were marked by quiet and serenity. Days of the rich and supreme pleasures of rendezvous returned a youthful zest to the spirit—the surge of joy at a reunion with an old, familiar face from hunting trails and battlegrounds long forgotten, gossiping with these old friends around talking and smoking fires and meeting new ones, bargaining with the traders for brand new things to hold and admire and be proud of; sharing the proud moments—and the bounty—with the women he loved.

In these fine thoughts, Walking Feather did not resent the white man's inroads; if it did not change from this through all the seasons, Walking Feather could be content and very accepting of his white brothers. Still, a dark corner of his mind told him this would not always be so. He felt the growing evil in his bones. The traders and other men along the river complained of the sinking beaver market in the East; the new white men coming into the country were more ruthless, more demanding and more brutal. Each boat up the river brought more; many came by land, on horses. Again, Walking Feather regarded it all with dismay.

His eyes came alert near him to the familiar face of a white trapper who had spent time in his village one winter and had frequently visited Walking Feather's lodge when Soft Wind and Grass Woman were small children. The old trapper made a sign of recognition and friendship to Walking Feather.

"Here is a white man I know," he said to his companions, as he returned the sign of greeting. "Hold my horse." He handed the reins to Standing Dog after getting down. "I will find out the news of rendezvous that will help us."

Between hand signs, Walking Feather's halting English, and the trapper's sketchy knowledge of the Crow tongue, the two traded questions and answers for several minutes while Standing Dog and the Shoshone watched stoic but expectant from their horses.

At last Walking Feather turned from the trapper smiling, and walked back to where they waited.

"We can return to our families and friends and urge them forward," he said, mounting his horse.

"What have you learned?" the Shoshone asked impatiently.

"There is much good to tell," Walking Feather said. "A young man rides ahead from my trusted friend Jacob Lyman who travels with the traders' mule train. This man, saying he is the son of Jacob Lyman's wife, has come here with word that Bad Hand and Griz Killer Lyman with many wagons will come before a second sleep. The white man's sickness kept them many days many miles to the east where the Platte joins the Missouri. I have heard talk that Jacob Lyman has taken a woman, but I do not know of these things."

The Shoshone spoke up angrily as they rode out of the rendezvous encampment. "Do these men bring the sickness with them? White men, I believe, carry evil spirits wherever they go. When they leave the villages of our people, the women wail and slash their arms in mourning because of the grief and death they bring!"

"The sickness has been left far behind," Walking Feather assured them. "My friend has told me that a white medicine man travels close to Griz Killer. His medicine was good for these wagon-train men cursed with the sickness. They would have died and the trading wagons never reached here. That he is a friend of Griz Killer is a sign that he is a good man. A shaman of the white man's God travels with them to teach the white man's ways to the Nez Perce and the Cayuse in the country far to the northwest. The white man's word for that far country is Oregon."

"More white man's evil," the Shoshone growled softly.

"No," Walking Feather assured. "I see it as a good sign. We must learn from these men and those who come among us to teach the white man's way and his religion. Then we will possess the medicine to have the kind of riches they now control that only come to us at the great price of many plews or the sacrifice of our horses or sporting with our young women."

"You talk nonsense, Walking Feather," Standing Dog protested. "The whites will never permit us the riches they control."

"Why then do they send medicine men and shamans among us if not to show us how to be rich as they?" Walking Feather argued.

Standing Dog looked at the Shoshone. "Our friend is hopeless. To him every day is sunshine and warmth and peace. He will learn. He will leave this rendezvous poor in spirit, shorn of his beaver for worthless trinkets and poorly made implements at great cost. His women will ride away from this time with the hairy faces with the sure knowledge that the key to all the white man's riches lies between their legs!"

Angrily, furious at their idle talk, and especially the idea that his wife and daughters were weak and would willingly go with the hairy-faced trappers, Walking Feather spurred his horse away from them to ride quickly to find his women and his horses and to urge them forward; he had had enough of the disturbing talk of the Shoshone and Standing Dog.

"Jacob Lyman will come!" he called back to them as he trotted his horse away. "He is a good man. He will speak straight to me of these things that will come to us."

Chapter Six

HAVING LEARNED THAT THE YOUNG COURIER TO THE rendezvous was Jacob Lyman's adopted son, Walking Feather set out, while his women erected the lodge, eager to find this young man and learn more directly from him about Lyman and the whereabouts of the wagon train of American Fur Company trading stock.

He was not hard to find, this youth in clean buckskin, good-looking for a white man. Walking Feather noted that Lyman's surrogate son owned a well-structured square-jawed face, a long and thin nose of almost noble proportions, blond hair, and deep and intense blue eyes above strong, ample cheekbones. Unlike most of the white trappers, his cheeks and chin looked as though as the sprouts of young manhood appeared, they were plucked and killed with clam-shell tweezers as many Indian youths did. Walking Feather was confused about this. Most white men carried sharp razors to shave daily or allowed their faces to fill with hair. The man Daniel, he knew from the talk of the land of Indian and trapper, had been an Indian captive and must have taken on many Indian ways. It pleased Walking Feather that Jacob Lyman's new son was so well-versed in the ways of his people. It drew Walking Feather even closer to his old friend, Jacob, and the woman he had not met, Jacob's new wife.

Still, sadly, in contrast to the lad's strong face, Walking Feather could see in the slight stoop of the young man's shoulders the weight of the yoke and the whip of his captivity; the dregs of evil and of guilt from his association with Thomas Penn and the blackguard Skull had not yet been fully purged.

In the midst of the clatter and noisy commotion of the trapper's celebration, he found Lyman's boy speaking with *Casapy*, "Blanket Chief" Jim Bridger, in white man's words Walking Feather had trouble understanding; he had learned many of the words, however, so got the gist of what they spoke. He stood away from them a respectable distance, eyes purposely averted, absently studying the rendezvous activity, hoping to give no one the impression he was there to overhear or to pry.

"Mr. Fontenelle turned the train over to Mr. Fitzpatrick at Fort Laramie," the young man explained in respectful tones. "Mr. Fontenelle rests there still weak from the trail sickness and the hardships of the journey from Bellevue."

Bridger's seamed and dour old-before-its-time face with its grimly clamped lower jaw was intent on Daniel's words. "Best, I reckon," he said. "Tom'd shine to getting 'em here faster. Lucien'll miss the Taos Lightnin' at ronnyvoo but I allow they's a passel of jugs at Laramie that coon'll root out fer hisself. The man's got hollow legs and feet like bufflerpaunch pouches when it comes to layin' up a cargo of that painter piss."

Bridger fished in his possibles bag to retrieve a burnt-out discolored old briar pipe. He ground a wad of tobacco to flakes with thumb and palm and tamped them down the charred, fire-eroded bowl rim.

"Hold still," he told the boy. He crouched at a nearby rendezvous fire, jerked out a flaming brand and touched it to the bowl, his cheeks collapsing as he sucked in his smoke to get the tobacco ember glowing. He trudged back, his head wreathed in pipe smoke, looking as though he had half swallowed the pipe as the battered bit was clenched deep in his back teeth with the fierce grip of a snapping turtle.

When he spoke it was with spit-slick lips working around the pipestem.

"Son, what's it I hear about a pair of them churchies ridin' with Jake and Tom?" he asked Daniel. His words came out harshly as if over a gravel bar.

"One of them is a preacher, Mr. Bridger, right enough. The other's of the church, too, but he's a doctor, looks after sick people. Reverend Parker they call the one. The other's Dr. Whitman."

"Do tell!" the burly Bridger exclaimed loudly, almost crowing in astonishment. "A honest-to-John boney-fidee sawbones with eastern official certificates and all such as that?! Not peddlin' snake-oil, is he?"

"No sir, That's what he is, Mr. Bridger—a regular doctor. Without him and his strong medicine, a bunch of those men working for Mr. Fontenelle wouldn't've got past the mouth of the Platte for the cholera. Mr. Fontenelle himself was bad sick. Three died as it was."

"Wall, I thank'ee, lad, for them encouragin' tidings that do this old coon's heart a heap of good. I'll be for havin' a palaver with this doctor first whack when the pack train gets in. If he's huntin' work, I got some for him."

While Daniel puzzled on that one, a genial-faced grinning trapper with eyes a-sparkle and with long black hair and a well-trimmed and debonair beard, strode past in beaded but well-worn and liberally smudged buckskins glossy in places from dirt and wiped grease. A flintlock Hawken rested casually along his left forearm, supported by the crook of his elbow and the grip of his right hand on the gun-wrist.

He walked with the jaunty step and body swing of a man in love with the world and full of lively mischief.

Bridger turned away from Daniel with almost impolite abruptness. "Here you, Meek!" he exclaimed, his head wreathed in vapor blown out of the pipe with sparks and embers over the emphasis of his words. "What the boys in your mess got on the fire?"

Joe Meek swerved in his determined course to come close to Bridger. "Fresh buffler, by dad, Gabe. Doc Newell and Dripps and some of them coons got prime tongue roastin' buried in the coals, hump ribs turnin' on the fire, *boudins* sausages sputterin' in the skillet. Fresh raw liver and gall for seasonin' to slick down your gullet for the prime fixin's, and Taos Lightnin' by the jugfull to wash her all down! You come by if you're of a mind, Gabe. But bring yer empty paunch. We-uns is fixin' to feed till we founder."

"I'll be by, hoss," Bridger promised. Turning back to Daniel with a sudden spin, Bridger affected a benign but faraway expression. "Wagh," he grunted, as if talking to himself. "I ain't et since yesterday and to boot I don't rightly recollect when. May've been afore the sun got high. In between this coon has counted coup on a sight of Taos Lightnin' at this here spree, or I'm poor bull." Bridger thoughtfully patted his belly. "And here's an empty paunch for Meek." He squared his shoulders, as if to get back to the business at hand.

"Son, I'll have my eye skinned for old Jake Lyman when Tom and them get in with the mule train. But you tell him if I don't see him right off, that Old Gabe hankers to see that medicine doctor first whack. Get that plumb center, now, boy!" His voice was so gruff, he sounded angry. Still his words were hardly meant to be intimidating; Daniel had quickly learned this was Jim Bridger's way and understood.

Before Daniel had a chance to respond, Bridger spoke again, breaking a grin around his tight-clenched pipestem. "You're a right smart kit coon, younker. You listen to your new pap, Jake. I'll warrant Jake Lyman'll shine when it comes to knowin' how to make a man of you or I'm poor bull!"

Again with a characteristic abruptness, Jim Bridger spun on his heel and stroke off on other business into the crowd of noisy, revelling mountaineers.

Walking Feather had waited patiently nearby until the young man became aware of him. Smiling, the one called

Daniel made a quick and clear hand sign of friendly recognition, which also surprised Walking Feather. He clasped his own hands in front of himself in a responding gesture of peace and greeting.

"You wish to talk with me? Are you Crow?" the young man asked in Crow dialect, and with a pleasant smile.

"Yes," Walking Feather responded. "I come to hear from you of my good friend, Jacob Lyman. I hear *Casapy* and others say you are Jacob's new son. That pleases me. I see he has a handsome man-child. You also use our words well and make the proper hand signs."

As Daniel explained having lived among the Plains Cheyenne and various mountain tribes as a captive, Walking Feather grew more pleased that he might have common talking ground with someone as much a kindred spirit as Jacob Lyman himself since Daniel was Jacob's adopted son. Having heard Blanket Chief Bridger speak of eating with Joe Meek, Walking Feather invited Daniel to his lodge that night to eat and talk, with the warm and welcoming hand and arm sign that "the robe is spread and the pipe is lit."

THE MAN SITTING near Walking Feather in his lodge—not much older than his own daughters, Soft Wind and Grass Woman—called himself "Daniel-england," a lot of whiteman name for Walking Feather to handle. Like Moon-that-Grows shortened to "Moon," the young man said he was best called "Daniel," which shorter name pleased Walking Feather.

The night before Griz-Killer Lyman was to ride in about midday with the trade-goods caravan guided by Broken-Hand Tom Fitzpatrick, Daniel sat on the south side of Walking Feather's lodge. He gingerly nursed a gourd bowl of scalding but nutritious stew of buffalo meat, fat and bone-marrow, flavorful and temptingly thick with locally gathered herbs, spices, seasonings, and wild onion, put together after the lodge was erected by Moon-that-Grows and her daughters.

Though the Indian lodges, clustered together regardless of tribe, were remote from the white-man rendezvous camp, the air around them still crackled with the roaring excitement and commotion of the celebrating trappers. Over that way, the night sky was pierced with yellow-bright light from the multitude of their big fires for talking, gaming, and drinking. Dark figures could be seen moving around and silhouetted against these fires. The loud talk, the shouts and the laughter of seemingly hundreds of drinking, carousing mountain men were only slightly muted by the lodge walls of wafer-thin scraped buffalo hide.

In each Indian lodge in the sprawling cluster, some distance away from the trappers' encampment in the peace of a soft night, a perfectly centered and small fire radiated a comforting warmth against the night's chill mountain air. Its smoke, as if heeding the call of the Great Spirit and prompted by a prevailing draft from under the skirt of the circular dwelling, spiraled languidly out the smoke hole at lodge-peak. Firelight through the parchment-like lodgeskins rendered the dwelling a tall, beckoning cone of thin yellow glow in the night, making vague, eerie shadows of movement within.

Across from Daniel, Moon-that-Grows and her daughters watched him expectantly, eyes gleaming with delight at the first visitor to their rendezvous quarters. They, too, were pleased to have a young and handsome white-man visitor so fluent in their language and with the messages of the hand-signs. Walking Feather explained to them that Daniel had learned these things as a captive of the Cheyenne and other tribes.

"Tell me of my friend, Jacob Lyman," Walking Feather asked the young messenger.

"The man I now call my father rides with Bad-Hand Fitzpatrick and the trading caravan not a day behind me.

Our family went east when the beaver fur lost its prime in the time of coming grass and long before rendezvous, so Jacob and my mother could find a white-man shaman—a preacher—to properly make her his wife."

"She escaped as a captive of the Cheyenne people," Walking Feather explained to his women. "Jacob Lyman saved her life when he killed a grizzly bear attacking her. It is still a legend around the white trappers' talking fires. Later she became Lyman's woman. He is now known as Griz Killer by the trappers and among our people."

"My mother's name is Rachel," Daniel said.

"Rachel," Moon repeated from where she sat across from him. "It is a good name, a good sound. I believe she is a good woman. A good mother." She looked at her smiling daughters as if they might not understand, but they did. "Rachel," she repeated. "Daniel's mother." Both young women nodded.

Soft Wind and Grass Woman looked at their mother and then at Daniel, smiling shyly in understanding. Both were pleasant for him to look at, but the smile and the gentle eyes of Soft Wind brought strange and embarrassing yearnings in his chest and in his loins. He quickly tore his eyes from her, feeling sheepish, guilty, and hoping Walking Feather did not read the story that must be written in his eyes and wrongly accuse him of having bad thoughts about Soft Wind and Grass Woman. Talk was an easy way to disguise the alien feelings spinning in his head and surging in special places in his body.

"Jacob found me with the evil white men named Skull and Thomas Penn and took me from them and to my mother," Daniel continued.

"Thomas Penn was killed and this Skull was sent east to be punished for making war on their white brothers for control of beaver lands," Walking Feather again explained for the benefit of the women. "These things we have heard. Thomas Penn tried to destroy Alexander MacLaren's Western Fur Company."

Daniel nodded, his head clearing now of the giddying cloud of fascination with Soft Wind's beauty. "Where the Platte River meets the Missouri we found the man Fontenelle with the white doctor Whitman caring for all the men of the trading caravan taken with the cholera sickness. We stayed to help them. A white shaman named Reverend Parker traveling with the medicine man Whitman made the ceremony that properly joined Jacob and my mother in the eyes of the white man's God."

"What of your first father?" Walking Feather asked.

"He was a white-man warrior chief killed by the Cheyenne when mother and I were captured and separated six summers ago."

The eyes of Moon, Soft Wind, and Grass Woman watching him with attention and wonder from across the lodge, melted with compassion. They knew of these things that sometimes happened to captives, white or Indian—but not in their village; Walking Feather's women felt it was wrong and cruel to ever separate loved ones for any reason.

"A young man such as you needs a father," Walking Feather declared. "You have had none for a long time. Jacob Lyman visited our village many times, along and with his trapper friend Rene Lamartine, a fine man who has been dead since the times of Thomas Penn's evil. I know Jacob. He will be a good father to you, Daniel. If sometimes he seems stern and harsh, remember he tries to make his best judgments about you and help you grow and be strong."

Daniel smiled at Walking Feather in recognition and understanding. He grinned inwardly at the irony. First Old Gabe Bridger and now Walking Feather had told him how fortunate that Jacob Lyman was his new father. Old men, he thought, must think that unwanted advice and caution to you is their bounden duty.

"Jacob has been firm, but never harsh," he said, sneaking another furtive look at Soft Wind and again sensing the start of mysterious cravings.

"Soft Wind and Grass Woman are unhappy at times with me," Walking Feather confessed.

Daniel saw the daughters study their father attentively.

"I will not always permit them the things they think are very special to have or to do. At the rendezvous, I tell them they must be careful not to be deceived by big-talk promises of the hairy-face trappers. These things are hard for a father to explain to his girl-children and become a worry."

Daniel had no way or reason to respond, so only looked across the short space past the fire that separated him from Moon-that-Grows and her daughters on the opposite side of the lodge ring. The last five or six of his eighteen years—until his reunion with his mother—had been turbulent and violent with no time nor opportunity to know friends of either sex of his own age. Forced into a role as a mindless dullard and camp tender for Skull and Thomas Penn, he had been otherwise coached in brutal, vicious behavior as a fighter and a killer by Skull, the man he had grown to look up to, depend on and—without the ability to distinguish right from wrong—came to accept as a savior and as a father.

Now, almost nine months since Jacob had rescued him, Daniel had begun to learn through his mother and foster father that there was goodness in the world. He began to understand that within himself there were special open places into his soul and within his heart for peace and tranquility and for deepening friendships with understanding and kind people such as he had found with Walking Feather's family.

He realized with a start that this warm family of Crow Indians were the first friends he had found on his own since his release from captivity. That sensation, too, filled his head and chest with giddiness.

These, he was also aware, were new and good feelings in his new time of life, as his sensations about Soft Wind were also new and good, and all these fine but unfamiliar experiences and sensations he needed time to ponder and understand.

His eyes this night in Walking Feather's warm and pleasant-smelling lodge, were drawn again to Soft Wind. Even her name was a calming influence. There was also a charm about Grass Woman, her younger sister beside her, but Daniel felt himself drawn more strongly toward Soft Wind.

"There's little here for me rendezvous," he explained, "than to be with my family while Jacob trades our beaver and talks with his friends. If Walking Feather has concern for Soft Wind and Grass Woman, I will walk with them in the rendezvous camp while you trade. They will like to see the happenings at the trading tables and watch the shooting contests and the horse races. They may find other friends here. No harm will come to them."

Chapter Seven

JIM BRIDGER SHOOED THREE WOOZY RENDEZVOUS CELEBRANTS away from a small fire, as with grim determination he hustled Marcus Whitman to it by the arm, looking back over his shoulder to make sure they wouldn't be disturbed or overheard. Dr. Whitman, lately arrived at the rendezvous camp and more amused by and humoring the crusty, insistent mountain man than anything, obediently consented to be led like a tethered goat. Jake Lyman had suggested as far back as their early conversations along the Platte that the legendary Bridger could be of considerable value to Whitman's plans in Oregon, and he was at last pleased with the chance to get acquainted with the fabled pathfinder.

Bridger crouched, motioning Whitman to get close to the fire near him. When the doctor hunkered down not far away, Old Gabe Bridger hitched himself almost annoyingly closer until they nearly touched.

Bridger abruptly reached out a hand to catch the back of Dr. Whitman's head and jerk it closer to his. Whitman complied, remaining amused over the eccentric behavior of the peculiar western trapper, guide, and legendary talespinner.

"Doctor," Bridger began, struggling weakly at normal speech after more than half a lifetime with the cryptic and perplexing mountain man's lingo. He spoke in hushed, confidential tones so no one would overhear. "I got somethin' I got a desperate need to take up with you." His voice and his eyes almost pleaded with Whitman, something odd for a man of Jim Bridger's reputation for being bold and aggressive as well as loud.

"At your service, Mr. Bridger," Whitman responded, looking into intense sky-blue eyes that had faced terrible death in a hundred ways, had fought, lived with and loved Indians, battled singlehanded the man-killing and giant beasts of the wild, western country, found the rivers and the passes, the paths and the trails around and over the frowning, forbidding mountains, and viewed the startling and bizarre wonders of Colter's Hell.

"Want to tell me about your problem?" He half-expected Bridger to unburden himself privately about a siege of hemorrhoids, the mountain man's "piles," for which he had soothing salves in his handy chest of supplies and medications.

"I can afford to pay you well, doctor."

"Where there is suffering, Mr. Bridger, I'm committed in service to my patient, to myself, to my profession, and to a merciful and generous God. Compensation is in a patient's recovery, good health, and gratitude. If there is payment to sustain the doctor's work, it is considerably after the fact, I assure you, Mr. Bridger. Now, sir, what is your problem?"

"It's a arrahead, Doc," Bridger blurted in sudden confession, cocking his head self-consciously, his face reddening with the revelation.

"A what?"

Bridger looked at him incredulously. "A arrahead! You know. Indian weapon. Two year ago it were, in a scuffle with the Blackfeet. I taken a Blackfeet arra inta my person, matter of fact two of 'em, but one of 'em's out and gives me no more miseries. But the other, after the fracas were over, stayed stuck down there yonder towards where I sit down, what we sometimes call the 'rear south.' A man's nether regions."

Bridger began to warm to his story and Dr. Whitman, a greenhorn in this country and with its people, listened with the rapt fascination of a man eager to understand and adjust to this new land, its attitudes, and its vagaries. He realized that with old Jim Bridger, he had on his hands both a nearly mythical and monumental giant of the New West, but as well a peculiar but common-enough sufferer with the miseries somewhere on his torso of an embedded "arrahead," and probably from what had already been said—and not said—in a sensitive, private zone.

Studying the man, Whitman judged him to be about his own age, possibly even a year or two younger, but with a roughened texture about him that made him appear at least a decade older. As some would observe of a man of his seasoning in life and his primitive bearing, "he was born old." And mountain men, he'd learned, tended to call good friends "old;" Bridger had already earned the nickname "Old Gabe." Maybe, Whitman thought with inward mirth, and thinking of the Old Testament, it was because Bridger did a pretty good job of blowing his own horn.

"Prithee continue, Mr. Bridger," he encouraged.

"A boy in our mess, a young thick-headed German coon name of Riehl . . . first names don't count for much out here, doc; they change with the wind . . . this Riehl—we called him 'Virginia' after the old-time dance, and for our particular brand of mountain man mischief, and because no one had caught hold of 'is proper first name. Well, Old Virginny, as we called him—he's long since been killed and skulped by the Pawnee—after that fracas with the Blackfeet, set about to yank them two arras out of my backside. Lord, he was rough! You know them bullheaded Germans whenever it comes to finishin' a job of work once started. Old Virginny was bound and determined he was gonna find that arrahead inside of me if it killed him, me, or both of us! Them arras appeared stuck there for good and all, I'm here to tell you. Old Virginny even propped a foot on my hind end to get proper purchase to yank at them arras! One were just under the hide and slid out slicker'n calf slobber with only a mite of bindin' in the meat because of the barbs."

Marcus Whitman shuddered convulsively with Bridger's graphic description, but was still beguiled by the raconteur's yarn, his head close to Bridger's by the dwindling mid-day rendezvous fire deep in the western Shinin' Mountains in the midst of the August, 1835, fur trappers' rendezvous as he listened with rapt attention. In these entrancing moments with Old Gabe Bridger, everything in Whitman's mind was set aside . . . the dream and the drama of a medical mission to the Oregon Indians; of his love for and visions of marriage and a future with the ravishing Narcissa Prentiss and their life and love and missionary zeal; the peevish Rev. Parker and of all the other peevishness of this often maddening quest to serve the cause of a loving God in a country ignorant of or oblivious to His great and merciful power.

Instead, his thoughts raced with the probable appearance of yet another chance to impress these men of the mountains. He recalled the shining, smiling faces of his former tormentors under Jake Lyman's shade arbor when he stood up as best man for the wedding of the mountain man and his devoted new wife.

But now Whitman's eyes centered on those of the great and legendary Jim Bridger, feeling this was a moment suspended in time and with an uncanny awareness of its significance to his destiny and of his own power now to manipulate that destiny and of Bridger's long established and special brand of legend, and history—and influence. With all of this spinning in his head, Dr. Marcus Whitman hung on the next revelation of the bleak-faced myth-man sitting next to him at the dwindling rendezvous fire.

Whitman sat quietly, watching and waiting, eyes searching his companion's, as Bridger regarded him intently, almost comically with those water-blue eyes that had seen the elephant. "The trouble is doctor, that the other'n slipped its moorings, naught else but shaft and gut wrappin's of the arrahead come out of that hole back down there. Old Virginny went at 'er like a Blackfeet out for blood with his Green

River knife, even lanced my hide and hams some more for a better look for it and that arrahead was buried beyond his reach. Lord, it pains me to recall it! After he'd dug around in my meat for what appeared a lifetime of misery, I allowed I'd had enough of his doctorin' for one day. And though it taken some persuasion, I got Old Virginny to call off the search and allowed we'd tackle her another time, and hain't got back to it since. Ner could I stand another butcherin' such as I taken from Old Virginny!"

Whitman was incredulous. "It's still in there?!"

"Yassir."

"Two years?"

"Yassir."

"The pain must be excruciating."

During his earlier recitation about "Virginia" Riehl, Bridger's voice had lost its pleading tone, to be replaced with almost a bravado as he warmed to his tale.

"Oh, I get so I don't pay it particular mind most of the time, doc. Sometimes she gives me the agonies of the damned. Like too long on a hoss and I commence to relive Old Virginny's cuttin' and pokin' and proddin' and pryin' with every lopsided, joltin' step of that cussed hammerhead. Cain't sleep on my backside neither or I'll forget and roll over and she'll twist in there and send me six feet straight up with a whoop in the middle of the night!"

"I'll have a look at it, but there's little I can do for you, Jim," Whitman confessed. "I have the proper surgical instruments and probes but nothing to dull the pain of such a major procedure. From what you tell me, it's buried deep. Laudanum wouldn't help in a surgical invasion so severe. They'll hear you scream all over this camp no matter what I give you to soften and mitigate the agony."

"Doc, you don't know me. Ner you don't know this kentry and what it can do for a man! I'll stand it, by God, never you mind. You're the first chance I've had to get her outten there clean and proper and I mayn't have another such chance again in this life. I don't want it in there another day. I'll pay whatever it takes."

"It offends me to the core, but I suppose I could knock you out with whiskey."

"Never you mind about that neither, doctor. I take whiskey in the shinin' times. This here ain't one of 'em. And I wun't abide laudanum. That's for pilgrims and green-horns and other such lily-livers and porkeaters. Let me take 'er like a man. A standin'-up, by-God, plews-and-parfleche hivernant mountain man! I'll not squirm ner scream, you have my word on that. And that's somethin' this coon's never gone back on. My word is precious; precious to me as my bond. Just that you have to do yer cuttin' and probin' in my lodge so's these curious ol' coons wun't have to see."

"But why all the secrecy, Jim?"

"Doc, you're new in this kentry. They's two things a mountain man cain't never abide. Never! Thet's never to retreat from a fair fight ner get snuck up on from behind."

"From what you tell me, these *were* wounds from a fair fight, or maybe with the odds against you. You didn't retreat, and they sure didn't sneak up on your backside!"

"Doctor, I've told some windies in my time around the night fires about where I been, and what I done, and what I seen. More to the point, these here old coons roundabout know everything I tell 'em is stretched a mite if not pulled plumb outta j'int. This one's true for a fact, but I most keep it to myself. No way it could be told proper."

"I still don't understand, Jim."

Bridger's voice turned almost shrill with insistence.

"That's what I been trying to tell you about you being a pilgrim that don't understand this kentry yet, doc, ner us hivernin' mountain men. Don't you see? Like I told you, them arras was stuck in my hind-end! How're them coons out there supposed to know I wa'n't skedaddlin' ner let myself get booshwhacked from the blindside!? Both of them's a sign of weakness or cowardice."

Whitman's mind went bright with inspiration. Bridger had revealed that a great deal more than pride was on the line. His own legend hung in the balance.

"Weakness!" he exclaimed. "You've carried that arrowhead inside you and suffered the agonies for two years and that's weakness? From what you tell me, Jim, you and Old Virginia and others were surrounded. That you're here today is testament that you fought your way out against a superior force."

"Was in a surround, by God!" Bridger chortled.

"No dishonor in that!" Whitman assured, watching and gauging Bridger's reaction.

"Nary a whit, Dr. Whitman." Bridger's usually grim-set mouth twisted into a grin with his pun, rare to a man of his directness.

"What's this 'hivernant' you speak of, Jim?"

"Why, son, that's a porkeater that ain't et but hawg, hominy, and hoecakes down on the farm afore coming in here to trap. If he lives long enough to get to his second ronnyvoo—or has wintered over, you might say—he can call hisself 'hivernant.'"

Mulling all that over, Whitman decided on a brazen gamble. Lyman told him he'd have to earn the esteem of the men of the Shinin' Mountains. Here was the chance to win Jim Bridger's eternal gratitude and esteem and to be the talk of the whole rendezvous encampment.

"Jim, if you say you could stand my opening the scar tissue and probe for the arrowhead in your lodge and not cry out or beg me to stop as you had to with 'Virginia' Riehl, why not show the world—and your cronies—once and for all what Jim Bridger's really made of and have me do it before the whole crew? Wouldn't you be about the greatest hivernant of all?"

Bridger blinked as he regarded Whitman soberly.

"I'd have to drop my drawers, doc. Out here, we're particular about showin' off our privates or our bare backsides."

"I'll put a cloak of some sort over you with a hole to expose only the area I work on. No one has to see more than that."

Bridger's still-questioning eyes suddenly turned bright. "Done, by beaver!" he enthused. "Give them ronnyvooin' coons somethin' to chew on over the night fires for years to come!"

Whitman exulted; he was well on his way to making his point, and perhaps, he thought, creating his own myth to match Old Gabe's.

"Bridger's legend is further assured!" he crowed. "I'll give you a day to draw a crowd, Jim."

Missing Whitman's attempt at humor, Bridger squared his shoulders. "Wun't take me that long, doc. I'll get Jake Lyman as your helper for your task. Joe Meek'll be my moral support. That there'll spread the word like wildfire! You got to get to know old Meek anyways, doc. He's got a pard we call 'Doc.' Robert Newell. Hell of a mountain man! You'll get to know all them coons. But Meek, now he's the best of the bunch."

Bridger's excitement was evident in his face as he became fully committed to the project.

"Doctor, Jake Lyman and his young Daniel has told me how them worthless mule train *engagees* wronged and abused you and that other churchy feller. And how you earned their undying respect by savin' the whole shebang of the ungrateful lot from the cholera back there on the Platte. I got a hunch this'll win you another big hashmark with these here hivernant mountaineers!"

Behind the broad grin of the greenhorn physician from New York State was a gloating glow. "Those are my sentiments exactly, Mr. Bridger!"

Chapter Eight

WITHIN AN HOUR AFTER JIM BRIDGER BROKE THE NEWS TO genial Joe Meek, word of the upcoming surgery—as Old Gabe predicted—became the talk of rendezvous, a celebrated event now eagerly anticipated, argued, and toasted from the ample supply of Taos Lightnin' or Mexican "awerdenty," the mountain man's efficient translation of the Spanish "aguardiente." Limited quantities of robust bourbons had come out from Kentucky for the discriminating and well-heeled mountaineer. Delicate brandies and smoky Scotch whiskeys were transported and sold for a stiff price by visiting booshways and trappers from the Queen Mother land north of the line, Hudson's Bay Company and sent by its chief factor, Dr. John McLoughlin.

Bridger's Challenge had spawned a new wave and surge of campfire chatter, celebration, and insobriety among the rough-and-tough-as-hell rustics who called themselves mountain men. Fresh jugs and bottles appeared everywhere to properly put dispositions into a merry mood for the next day's event. The rising crescendo of rendezvous euphoria was apparent to Jake Lyman as he strolled the camp in search of Mark Whitman. The lateness of the American Fur Company caravan coupled with dire news of the sagging beaver market out East and the staggering increase in prices for trade goods had dampened the usual no-holds-barred raucous gaiety and enthusiasm of rendezvous; now a new, vigorous spirit burst forth into full bloom as the roar of celebration swelled another octave.

By early evening, Jake had heard about Bridger's Challenge—removal of the "arrahead with nary a whimper"—in separate, lively encounters. Typical of the fur frolic as Taos lightnin', the wild wagering and the night-fire auguring sessions began almost immediately in deadly earnest. A few alcoholic shouting matches and fist fights broke out between Bridger loyalists and the surgery skeptics, but luckily no one was stabbed or shot. The betting stakes were measured in beaver plews, and in many cases, the results of a year's suffering and labor were laid on the line—to hell with needed trade goods. "Hell, hoss," was the cry, "this hyar's ronnyvoo! Hyar goes hoss an' beaver!"

The question: Would Old Gabe Bridger endure the ordeal stoic or screaming? Because of his declaration to the already respected Dr. Whitman that he would take the cutting and the digging like a man, the odds quickly leaped five to one in favor of his bellering his fool head off. Self-styled soothsayers lurked behind every rock and tree. The multitude of crackling and sparking rejuvenated rendezvous night-fires were a-buzz; would he or wouldn't he?

Word quickly got out about the patient himself and certain grimacing bettors began to doubt their wisdom: The object of all the furor who held in the grip of his jaw the decision over his reaction to the agonizing surgery, was the heaviest investor in his own behalf—Jim Bridger. Those who had wagered heaviest against him began wearing long faces and looking at one another perplexed.

But tomorrow was another day. As the gloaming settled over the noisy and sprawling rendezvous camp, Jake Lyman resumed his search for Dr. Marcus Whitman in a lodge Tom Fitzpatrick had arranged for Whitman and for Rev. Parker as a courtesy and token of appreciation of the American Fur Company for Whitman's medical miracles at Bellevue.

Trudging through the gathering murky, smoke-stained dusk, Jake Lyman grew more aware of the nostalgic, familiar—and comforting—sights, the sounds and the smells of rendezvous, as alone he hiked the encampment sprawl. In the dwindling gray light, the vast valley before and around him was a blur of impressions of men paused to talk or in buzzing clusters in nearby and far-off activity, a seething of humanity close up as well as in a broader, overall view.

Happily resurrected night fires resumed their glow in the vastness of the dipping, rising valley as eager yellow flame-fingers probed hungrily into the coming darkness. Distant Indian lodges along the fringes of rendezvous turned again into warm and compelling yellow cones of human occupancy from the dancing fires inside backlighting thin-scraped lodge covers.

All around him, Lyman was conscious of a tempo, a beat—akin to a musical score—rough and lopsided to be sure, but a measured, busy rhythm in the hum and the roar of men and talk and rendezvous and reunion, the mumblings and the words and the shouts, the axe thuds on seasoned, dry squaw wood for night fires, the rattledy-clack of straw-thin lodgepoles tips lofted into place as camp was made and the rhythmic tapping of pegs to tether lodgeskin skirts. Interspersed as another percussion cadence in this symphony of encampment came the hollow thunking sound as fur company *engagees* drove wedges into the fur presses of the mountain-stream commerce tightly forging the rendezvous bounty of beaver plews into fiercely compressed, impersonal bales for the trip east. This was the mill-grist that company men and free trappers had suffered and toiled and risked a year of their lives in gleaning. Now, the accumulated bales' embarkation would wistfully herald the end or beginning of the end of rendezvous and the goodbyes and the start of another dangerous, desolate year. But rendezvous was now, and here and there Lyman's concerto was punctuated by a happy halfstock Hawken or a Leman or a Tryon big-bore taking one last shot at the mark before dark, or just into the sky in jubilation or inebriation. Lyman clearly distinguished the snappish bark of a St. Louis or a Pennsylvania rifle as brighter than the jackass cough of a Hudson's Bay Northwest smoothbore fusil or "fuzee."

Natural, human, and animal smells merged to be sorted by his sensitive nostrils to add to his relishing of his rendezvous roundelay—the sharp, not always unpleasant, aroma of unwashed bodies packed too close together in buckskins that hadn't been off—or for very long—and greasy hair that hadn't seen water, in a year. What met Jake's nose was more a pervasive and overriding masculine musk melded of squaw-mounting scents, of cooked meat and fat and marrow, the bladder-gall and spattered blood of the buffalo-butcher, medicine-musk glands and honest sweat and long hours and from buckskins sodden in beaver ponds or by torrential rains baked and shrunk brittle but warmly liveable again over night-fires in the high rocks, on frigid stream banks, or at the buffalo chip "prairie coal" smolderings of the flatlands. The men of rendezvous had come from all points of the compass, high, low, in-between, go-to-hell, and all been-to-the-mountain. "Seen the elephant," as a mountain man would say of the experience. To Lyman's senses, the smells as well merged and blended in the here-and-now scent of rendezvous wood fires and their varied smoke, mellow and savory or with eye-watering astringency, and of the kinds and care and preparation of fresh game—antelope and buffalo parts—broiled, baked, or just simply blackened for the celebrants; of the rich mustiness of brittle and broken winter-cured grass or the moist appeal of the trampled and crushed verdant and succulent blades of summer, and of the nose-clogging powder-dust pounded pemmican-like and churned up to swirl in haunting dust-devils against a prevailing wind where already horse-forage was nibbled and hoof-pawed to oblivion, and where hurrying mountaineer moccasins had beaten irregular hill-side-perched trails to jovial companionship or the privacy of a piss. Blended with the wind-borne dust was the ever-present biting smell of urine, the strongest of it animal, and of manure, the least tolerable whiff of it, man's.

Darkness drenched and enriched the land and in these moments, Lyman's heart was good as he entered a lodge to find Dr. Whitman rearranging the handy portions of his transported medical utensils and medicines carried in a brown leather-bound wood hand chest of eastern manufacture. Rev. Parker was absent.

"I may have bitten off more than I can chew, Jake," Whitman confessed as he recognized Lyman stepping into the lodge's bleak firelight.

"I'd say you have, Mark. But that's your doin's and nothing to what Jim Bridger's bit off!" Lyman responded. "Sad— or happy—to say, you've set yourself up for establishing or destroying your reputation among the mountaineers depending on how things go tomorrow."

"He wanted to do it today, Jake, but finally allowed that I was probably trail-weary and would appreciate the chance to bathe and shave, eat and have a good night's rest. All of which, but the latter, I've done. We'll attend to his errant 'arrahead' tomorrow."

"What a shrewd old coon," Lyman observed, glancing around the well-ordered lodge. "There's a method to Old Gabe's madness," he went on. "That man could sell quillwork and baskets to Indians. As I get it, if he endures it tomorrow without screaming for mercy, he'll own about two thirds of this camp by afternoon!"

"It takes some crazy kind of logic and courage to want this procedure out here under these conditions. He'd really best go east to a proper hospital, maybe in St. Louis and have it surgically and properly attended to under sanitary conditions. And I should have refused to consider it out here. In all this filth. But now I'm stuck with the challenge and so is he!"

"You both will win, Mark. If Old Gabe cries out in pain, he loses. And he's wagered about everything but scalp and hide on being able to take it. If he loses his grit and cries out, he loses it all, including esteem. He'll wind up having to

take work scraping hides with squaws to get by. No, it'll
work, Mark. Jim'll rise to the occasion. I'd personally make
a side bet with you that on the morrow Jim Bridger will
redeem himself . . . and you!"

"I'm not a betting man, Jake, but you seem uncommonly
confident of Jim's nerve in the face of more agony than one
man deserves."

"I've got inside information," Lyman said with a sly smile.

"What's that?"

"From the best judges of all whether Jim can pull it off,
Mark. All of his close friends, Meek and Newell, Andy
Dripps and Fitzpatrick, and some others, ones who've
known him and trapped and made camps and traveled and
caroused with him for years and know Jim Bridger best . . ."
Lyman paused for effect.

"Yes?"

"They waited till the odds got out of sight and then they
started staking everything they own on Jim."

Chapter Nine

AT PRECISELY NINE O'CLOCK IN THE MORNING—THOUGH THERE
were few watches in the crowd to consult—on the thirteenth
of August, in the year of our Lord, eighteen hundred and
thirty five, in the valley of the New Fork of the Green River
deep in the celebrated Shinin' Mountains of the Great
American West, Jim Bridger stepped out of his lodge with
great flourish. He confronted a crowd of cheering—and
some drunkenly jeering—mountain men and stoic, stone-
faced but inquisitive Indians.

The Indians had heard that one of the first true white
medicine men they'd ever seen or heard of was this morning
to perform what they considered a miracle on Blanket Chief
Bridger, a man many of their people respected—and an
even greater number feared.

As he regally emerged into the sunlight to appraise the
throng surrounding him, Bridger—living up to that Indian
name, "Blanket Chief"—was cloaked neck-to-hock in a brand-
new and thick Hudson's Bay blanket of eye-smarting crimson
with wide, broad, and rich black edging. Near his right flank, a
hole, four-inches in diameter, had been cut into it to facilitate
the surgeon's work. The blanket was gathered and clutched to
his chest; his feet were adorned with gorgeous, new beaded
moccasins of colorful Sioux design and manufacture.

Around him the pressing, noisy throng courteously
formed a great thirty-foot-round space in respect to patient

and surgeon. Mountaineers stood in ranks, three, four, and five men deep. So everyone could see, the taller stepped back of the medium-sized. Those of average build, in turn, gave way to the short men in the front rows, affording nearly everyone a good view. Only a few in the far back had to crane their necks. Along the inner rim, a few knelt, crouched, squatted or sat cross-legged.

Ominous as a waiting guillotine, a jury-rigged operating table stood stark in its simplicity in the open sunlight, and coldly sinister in its function. Two broad and thick oak planks supported by enormous waist-high whiskey barrels that served as a trading table had been lent by one of the traders, as commerce had wisely adjourned for the surgical ceremony occupying nearly everyone's attention.

Taking his place beside Jim as he popped out of his lodge, Joe Meek, like a dueler's second, fell into step on the ceremonial march toward the waiting torture rack. Apart from his colorfully beaded and begrimed buckskins, the debonair Meek was gaily caparisoned in a thick red-wool knit voyageur's cap, its long, tapering top and knot rakishly dangling over one ear, and a matching bright-red, wide, finger-woven wool sash with accents of eye-catching yellow yarn, knotted at the side of his waist, the streamers and tied fluff-ends dangling to his knee.

Ceremoniously held high for all to see as Meek marched with Bridger to the table, was a two-inch wide, six-inch length of quarter-inch thick parfleche—dense rawhide dried to the consistency of cast iron—Bridger's only concession to the coming agony. Like the bitten bullet in battlefield surgical invasions and amputations without anesthetic, he'd clench it in his teeth against the pain as Whitman plied his scalpel and probes.

Opposing bettors had already agreed to other compromises; the surgeon was permitted to occasionally confer with his struggling patient without them calling "foul."

The onlookers courteously made way as a bareheaded Dr. Whitman—almost like an opposing duelist in crisp white shirt and tight-fitting buckskin trousers—with Jake Lyman at his side in full buckskins, emerged out of the crowd to walk with measured tread toward the table from the opposite side. Also resembling a duelist's second, Lyman formally carried Whitman's leather-bound surgical hand chest under his arm like cased dueling pistols.

In the spread of warm morning sunlight of rendezvous, the two principals and their subalterns met at opposite sides of the rude operating table.

"Mr. Bridger," Dr. Whitman greeted.

"Dr. Whitman. A good marnin' ta ya, sir."

"My assistant, Mr. Lyman," Whitman said.

"We're acquainted," Bridger responded, reaching across to shake Jake's hand. "It's been a while, Jake," he said, also shaking Whitman's hand. "My associate, Mr. Joseph Lafayette Meek."

Meek's eyes sparkled in mirth, relishing the mock formalities. "We've not met, Dr. Whitman," Meek said pleasantly, extending his hand across the table. "It's my extreme pleasure. You saved some of my friends back on the Platte." Shaking hands with Dr. Whitman, he swung his proffered handclasp to Lyman. "I'm told congratulations are proper, Jake. I look forward to meetin' Miz Lyman and yer new son. Hear tell he's changed some for the better of late. We all know the story and we're puffed with pride that you're one of us hivernants."

"My respects, Joe," Lyman said softly. "Rachel and Daniel both are right over there, yonder to your left. Standing with the family of my friend Walking Feather of the Crows."

Meek glanced at them, smiled, and back at Lyman, tightened his eyes and grinned in comradeship for their shinin' times in rendezvous' past. He gave Lyman's hand a second, strong grip.

"Mr. Bridger," Whitman spoke up for the moment of truth. "Shall we proceed?"

"Get at it, doc!" Bridger cheered loudly, jubilantly waving at the crowd and hoisting his rump to the table and rolling onto it. In an ungainly hands-and-knees pose on the table, the crimson blanket draped like a tent, he again spoke up. "Them's my final words till Doc Whitman takes his last stitch! Then I'll beller all I damned please!"

"We'll howl with ya, Jim!" someone yelled out of the now-silent crowd and a ripple of approving laughter followed it.

A heavy hush came over the bystanders and, paradoxically, over the land—not a breath stirred—as Bridger flopped prone, resting the side of his head on his crossed arms. Whitman adjusted and tucked the blanket gently around Bridger so its prearranged hole exposed the large shiny purplish lumpy, pocked and puckered scar of Ol' Virginny Riehl's hasty unsutured battlefield surgery. Joe Meek stood close to Jim's head with the slab of parfleche ready when Jim needed to chaw on it. Lyman waited beside Whitman with abundant rolls of snow-white gauze to staunch the flow of blood as required.

"Now or never," Whitman muttered, poising the scalpel and, guessing that the ugly scar represented proximity to the "arrahead," began, laying a quick, long and bloody incision along it. Bridger's head trembled on its stiffened neck and rammed itself deeper into his crossed hands without a murmur.

The wound was deepened and the patient's body convulsed mildly as the surgeon's scalpel sought contact with the buried object. Bridger at last beckoned for the parfleche and gripped it deep between his straining jaws. Whitman motioned to Jake for pads of gauze and dabbed at the freely oozing carmine blood to maintain proper visibility.

The incision deepened, he called for his probe; Whitman was sweating now, the once well-brushed hair dangled down his forehead and was pasted in the beads gathering there. His shirt back was stained with sweat.

In he went with the probe and Bridger's body violently jerked. A massive sigh of awe and respect rolled over the onlookers in unison.

Whitman straightened. "I found it," he murmured in relief to Jake and only the front rank of spectators overheard. He turned back to his work, peering intently into the deep and bleeding incision. "Dear God!" he was heard to say with a gasp.

He leaned near Bridger's head, now swollen and purple in the immense strain of control and jaw-grip on the now-mangled parfleche. Tears of his endurance glistened on his cheeks.

Whitman, his voice choked with emotion and urgency, spoke quickly but softly. "I've found it, Jim. Something I hadn't expected. It's embedded in the bone——"

"Get it outta there, doc," Bridger pleaded, his words grunted and strung together, "I cain't hold it much longer."

"I can't, Jim," Whitman said, his voice cracking in emotion. "It's buried," he moaned. "It's a metal arrowhead and apparently when the shaft was yanked on, it bent back like a fish hook. Jim, I don't have the tools. I think . . ."

"God damn you, Whitman!" Bridger's voice rose shrilly in his agony. "I said get it out of there! If it takes goin' in with a hammer and chisel. Finish your work, man!" His final sentence, though choked and strained, was shouted and all heard.

Joe Meek looked across at Jake Lyman, his eyes streaming with helplessness. Lyman grit his teeth, clenched his eyes and shook his head in response.

Whitman also looked at Lyman, a pleading depth in his eyes, but also with the wild look of a man driven. "I guess these forceps, Jake. They're the best I've got. It's fused in there with cartilage and calcified. I'm sure it won't budge."

Lyman was fired with inspiration. He leaned forward and whispered in Whitman's ear. "You'll do it, Mark. Three gods depend on you—Jim Bridger, Jesus Christ, and God Almighty!"

With a wad of his gauze, Whitman took a moment to dab at his streaming forehead and to look quickly at the hushed, expectant crowd. Forceps in hand, he sent another glance at the cloudless sky. "Give me strength, Lord," he muttered. "Give me the courage of this man, my patient!"

With that he eased the forceps into the wound; Bridger's body set up a violent trembling that rattled the oak-plank tabletop.

"I've got it," Whitman finally muttered through gritted teeth. "Caught hold of it." He tightened his grip on the forceps handles. "Now, Jim. Get a good bite on your leather. She's coming out! I have to push down hard to release the hook and break through the solid matter that holds it secure. Take a grip!"

Bridger's body tensed for the final agony. Whitman pushed against the instrument in his hand, his own arm shaking with the strain. "It's loosening," he grunted hoarsely after long seconds of prying and forcing. "I can feel it wiggle." Bridger's head now thumped hollowly and involuntarily against the planking, his face bloated with blood and purple. His eyes, when he opened them, were a bloodshot crimson.

"It's coming. I can feel it. Just a few more wiggles. Any second now." Whitman managed a slow back and forth motion of the forceps. "Here it comes. Once . . . more. Agh!" His hand jerked with the release and he quickly retrieved the dripping forceps with the equally dripping red arrowhead in the jaws. Tossing the mess on the table, he signalled to Jake for his surgical needle and stitching thread, already prepared.

"You won't notice this hardly at all, Jim, after what you've been through." His patient now lay silent.

"Jim?" Whitman called again. The man lay inert, unmoving. Whitman checked his pulse and pressed his ear to his back, listening to Bridger's racing heart and his heaving lungs. "Jim? He may have passed out."

"I'm here!" Bridger growled loudly. "Get the gawdam job done!"

Relieved and smiling, Dr. Whitman turned to the work of stitching up his incision and preparing a dressing. At last it was finished.

"We're through, Jim," he proclaimed jubilantly. "You can howl now!"

"Hain't got the stren'th," came the muffled voice of the man with his head still on his arms. "You boys'll have to help me up."

Jake Lyman raced around the table as Joe Meek tried to support a shaky Bridger sitting at the edge. Together they helped hold him. His face now pale and drawn, he weakly surveyed the crowd again.

"Well, boys," he said, his voice shaking. "I done 'er, by beaver! I won!"

A cheer went up from the crowd that rattled the lodgepole tips of Bridger's nearby tepee. Everyone was jubilant; even the losing bettors felt they'd gotten their money's worth.

Dr. Whitman was also quickly at Jim's side, watching his face and eyes for after-effects and checking his pulse again and his heart-rate. "Want that arrowhead for a souvenir, Jim?"

"Nah, throw the dratted thing away! I lived with it two years and like a spiteful woman, I want it outta my sight!"

"I don't know, Jim," he said. "I don't know how you lived with it. Don't know why infection didn't kill you."

Bridger mustered his first grin since climbing up on the table.

"Doc, that's somethin' else you gotta learn out here. The air in this kentry is so pure, meat just don't never spoil!"

His brave and bright response brought another roar of acclaim from the assembled mountaineers.

Chapter Ten

JAKE LYMAN FELT THE GNAWING DEEP IN HIS BONES. THE rendezvous' high sunlit plateau of jubilation and celebration over Jim Bridger's triumph of sheer guts and will under Marcus Whitman's knife quickly sloped away to a dark valley.

The old styles were changing and it was as plain to Lyman as if it had been written in the sky in large black letters.

Around the campfires, the burden of change lay heavy in the talk around him. Where in the early hours of rendezvous the fire rings resounded with hilarious whoops, lively laughter, and talk that was mostly senseless jabber, conversations now turned low and muted and measured with frequent silences as men stared into the flames, cloaked in thought.

Much as the mountain men welcomed and respected the bold and chipper New York doctor and tried to understand his solitary, sometimes sullen-appearing preacher-companion, these outlanders and others swarming in from the East augured ill of things to come. The tall Shinin' Mountains and the fur trappers' beloved vast, solemn lands were losing their virgin feel. It had begun to smell tainted, this land, its freshness never to return for those who had seen it first, broken the trails and tapped the wealth of uncharted beaver streams. Lyman knew it was a feeling of jealousy, the code of first-come rights. The trappers also knew they were powerless against what promised one day sooner or later to be like a tidal wave of humankind.

Around the fires, Jake also heard the bitching tongue of blame; the big companies, the government, the emptyheaded easterners pouring in, were, in their eyes, responsible and they trumpeted the sour notes loud and clear.

Other buckskinners disregarded the bleak omens that rode in this year with the fur company wagon trains from the East. They went heedlessly on with the drinking and the shooting and the carousing and coaxing Indian girls into the thickets for a handful of cheap but colorful trade beads.

Others responded to the dark tidings with despondency, incapable of creative response, sitting away alone, staring morbidly into the mouth of a jug.

Rachel waited for Jake in a lodge Fitzpatrick provided in gratitude, one of several Broken Hand freighted in from Fort Laramie for company use and storage or housing for his *engagees*.

"Where's the boy?" Jake asked as he stooped to step through the small, circular entry. Their gear and folded sleeping robes lay clean and orderly around the lodge's perimeter. A small, dancing fire centered directly under smoke flaps propped open to welcome sky and breeze above gave a lift to Lyman's dragging spirits.

"Daniel's found decent friends in Walking Feather and his wife and their daughters. He went there to eat with them and take Soft Wind and Grass Woman on a walk through the camp and down along the river."

Impulsively, Lyman strode to embrace his wife for a long, loving kiss. "We don't get many chances any more to be alone," he said softly.

"Now's not a good time," she whispered, her mouth close to his ear, feeling her own urges rising in response to her husband's. "Never know who may poke his head in the door."

"We could take a long walk late this afternoon into those hills along the river," Lyman suggested. "I'm not much worried about hostiles with so many trappers and friendly Indians about."

"It's been a long time," she murmured.

"What there was was always risky with Daniel so close."

"Later," came Rachel's whispered promise as she drew away from him. "In some ways, in our relationship, he was in the way. Still, I am so everlastingly grateful that he's been returned to me. I think he's making marvelous progress, don't you?"

"Yes, but he still bears watching. Walking Feather will be a good influence if they become friends. He was so generous with me years ago. Something bothers me, and I might as well say it. I watch it cautiously, but I believe Daniel's developing a fondness for Soft Wind."

"I've seen it too. Why do you say cautiously? Is there something wrong with honest feelings?"

Lyman studied his new wife. Perhaps in her joy of reunion with her long-lost son, she was blinded to Daniel's weaknesses.

"Rachel, less than a year ago, he was ridiculed with the name 'Orphan' and abused and humiliated in five years of captivity and becoming the unwitting disciple of villainy at the feet of that master demon, Skull."

"But he's responded so well. To you, Jake. To us."

"From where he's been and for so many years, it's a long road back to decency, Rachel. His formative years were under cruel, demeaning people who did nothing constructive for him. For my part, I've granted his freedoms slowly, as he's earned them. I've praised goodness and tried not to be critical—well, not overly—of lapses. He'd forgotten what freedom and responsibility stood for. He has to learn gradually their bearing on a happy, fulfilling life."

"I know, Jake. I love you for stepping in so caringly to take Edwin's place as a firm but concerned father."

Lyman went to sit on a pile of buffalo robes that made up their bedding. "I think we still have a fragile truce with the rascal that Skull plotted to encourage. I'm just not sure, Rachel, if he's fully ready for any deepening relationship with Soft Wind. Or any woman. I do know this. His interest in Soft Wind, if such it is, won't be a passing thing based on momentary lust. I don't fear that. But a man–woman commitment is a vow for life. Or it better be if I have any say in the matter."

"We may be crying wolf too soon, Jake. I understand you and your concerns. Mine are the same, but let's not judge in haste. Let's cross those bridges later . . . Jake?"

He looked over at Rachel, crouched in her buckskin dress, looking more Indian than white herself, as she poked at the fire and added short lengths of gray, cured tree limb to rejuvenate the blaze.

"Something about you since we've been here," she said. "Different. There's more on your mind than Daniel's apparent infatuation with Soft Wind."

"It shows?" he asked.

"Sometimes you've been silent and deeply thoughtful. You're always good about telling me what's on your mind. I feel it elsewhere at this encampment, too. Something's in the air. The sun shines here, but there's a dark cloud in it somewhere."

Lyman studied his wife with an awe that transcended his love; with her knack for reading between the lines, she'd be a hard person to deceive. Despite her perplexity over the trend of things, he chuckled inwardly at her intuition.

"It's nothing, really, to bother you about. It's trapper business. But if you've seen a change in my attitude that worries you, then I suppose I'd ought to tell you about it. There's been unsettling news from the East. All this is hard to explain. What's happening is as tough as smoke to get a grip on and hold up to the light. It's many-sided and it's thorny. This life of ours—the trade of the fur hunter—is in jeopardy."

He considered for a moment how to tell her. How much of it would Rachel really be interested in?

"Things are changing—considerably. In almost every detail. It affects all of us. Fur's been a major cornerstone of

America's—and Canada's—economy since long before men ventured west of the Mississippi."

He paused again.

"We—these men around us at rendezvous—have reached the point we're trapping the beaver out. Much more of the rampant harvest we've enjoyed for years and there just won't be any beaver left. To add to that, the market for beaver fur out east is gravely troubled, so the price is plummeting. For years, beaver was the only pelt for making formal dress hats, and the winter-prime underfur of beaver was the major factor in the making of felt for hats. That's all changing. They've machines now for making felt of passable quality from rabbit, nutria, and even cat!"

Rachel watched him intently. "End of an era in the making? I begin to see your concerns," she said, her eyes studying his.

"We've another unsettling development to deal with. The Chinese."

She looked at him quizzically, but remained silent.

Lyman grunted. "Huh! Back to more history. The opening of a trade route with the Far East was the goal of the search for a Northwest Passage. Exploration of the great American West, really, was only something that happened along the way. Finding the abundance of beaver was secondary to the challenge to discover easy passes over the Shinin' Mountains, or a fabled navigable river that would link east and west. Much of that began in earnest thirty or more years ago under the Jefferson administration and with the grand captains, Lewis and Clark. The mythical river route turned out to be just that. In chasing the wealth in beaver, though, men like Bridger and Jed Smith and Joe Walker all but found the mountain passes and the easy trails to finally connect the links to bridge the continent. The beaver men did it and even as they did it, it was their undoing."

"You talk in circles and over my head, Mr. Lyman," Rachel chided lovingly. "What do you mean, 'undoing'? And what did you mean about China?"

"Don't you see? These mountain men marked out and widened the trails through the very country they loved because it was so awesomely beautiful but so damnably inhospitable. Reversing the old saw by beating a path to the door of the Orient where they're building a better mousetrap. Or you might say, are killing off the beaver!"

He grunted with the irony of his metaphor, and Rachel regarded him with a puzzled expression.

"The Chinese, the Far East," he explained looking at her with mystery in his eyes. "And their damned silkworms!"

"Silkworms?"

"It defies the imagination. There's the nub of the low mood of this rendezvous, Rachel. Silkworms! I thought it was another of Bridger's campfire windies. But he could never dream up a yarn like this."

Staring thoughtfully into Rachel's now crackling lodge fire, Lyman again grunted at an unintentional metaphor.

"To hear Bridger tell it, the Chinese silkworm is like our caterpillar. But different. The strands the silkworm spin into the cocoon are longer and tougher. The Chinese have learned to unravel the filaments, spin them into a fine thread which they weave into a delicate but durable fabric called silk."

"What's that got to do with it, Jake?"

"That's just it. Edging the beaver out. Man's high-fashion hats in silk are running beaver hats a close race in the market. So, as demand for beaver pelts drops, so does the value. Felt makers turning to less desirable fur chops at it, too."

Lyman bit his lip in thought and stared into the fire. Still at the fire ring, Rachel watched him without comment.

"It's vicious, all of it. Not just one thing. The combination of all of it."

"How do you mean, Jake?"

"About the only reward for this miserable and lonely trapper's life is that this splendid, savage country is about as close to heaven as you'll find this side of the line. The vexing part is that the fur companies get rich twice off the company men and the free trappers way out here—and of course, gouging the Indians even deeper—by buying low and selling high in both plews and in trade goods."

Lyman paused again, his drift of thought reflected in his eyes as Rachel listened intently. "And there's jolly little we can do about it."

"I don't understand."

"It's simple. As cruel as it is, it's simple. Beaver plews delivered in St. Louis fetch more than a hundred to a thousand percent over what the trapper got in credit at rendezvous. Likewise the price of staples, whiskey, and trade goods freighted to rendezvous cost more than a hundred to a thousand percent more out here than out east. The trappers put up with it because they love the life and would have no other. But now that's changing and changing fast as the beaver market goes to hell. The companies can't be expected to budge. To them, it's to hell with this western country and its charms. To them it's just a means to an end—money. When their profits slump in the fur market they make up for it by gouging the trappers with jacked-up prices for supplies and trade goods."

"What my father would have called a vicious circle," Rachel responded.

Lyman looked at her, agreement in his eyes. "Damned near laughable," he mused, unamused. "If it weren't so shamefully pathetic."

For a long moment he stared up at the blue sky through the lodge's flared smoke hole. "Then there's our Indians, simple as children for the most part. And I don't say that unkindly, Rachel. They've developed the most efficient living imaginable. They take nothing more from the land than they put back. They are careful never to eat the seed corn. But white man's greed, like his whiskey, poisons their minds with unreal images. Because they are not familiar with insincerity, they are many times more the victims of all this than the trappers!"

He got up and went to her by the fire. Rachel stood up and he took her in his arms. "That, in a long way round, may account for my disposition of late, Rachel. I thank God for you in my life, your willing influence, and openness in sharing my burdens."

Rachel pulled back, reluctant as yet to let the matter rest.

"And I love you, Jacob, for the same reasons and more. If I may be permitted an observation, it's not the problem, Jake, so much as how you deal with it."

"I don't understand."

"Nothing is ever all black and all white, Mr. Lyman, The question is how will you let it affect your life? And mine. And Daniel's."

"I figured there wasn't a great deal I could do about it."

"Nonsense! You can let it destroy you or you can find the means to cope with it and grow, Jake. And I don't mean by joining the greedy and the manipulating. There must be a way of riding out the rough times in dignity."

"Times have always been rough one way or another, whether it's out east or back here. And you've surely endured perilous times and abided," he acknowledged.

"Then what's so different about this? Have you spoken with Mr. Bridger and Mr. Fitzpatrick?"

"They told me about all this. They don't have any answers."

"What about Dr. Whitman?"

Lyman was dumbfounded. "Rachel, Mark Whitman is without experience in this country and in matters like this. He'd be no help at all."

"Of course not. Not until you explain it to him as you just did to me. Jake, Dr. Whitman is an educated, intelligent—if not brilliant—man of considerable experience in his own right. What harm could there be in speaking with him? His mission sponsors in his church consider him to be of sufficient character and stewardship ability, else they wouldn't finance his missionary venture in the Oregon country. Sometimes we're blinded to solutions by being too close to the problem. Dr. Whitman admires and respects you and enjoys your company, Jake. I've seen it in his attitude around you . . . when he consented to serve as your groomsman at our wedding and in seeking you out to assist him in his ministering to Mr. Bridger."

Jake thought about Rachel's powers of observation and her very pointed wisdom.

"Well, just for the fun of it, I'll have a talk with him. You have a way of helping me get things off my chest and seeing things more clearly, and so does he."

Chapter Eleven

SINCE COMING TO RENDEZVOUS, DANIEL ENGLAND HAD experienced so many new and delightful sensations that his head and chest virtually ached, they were so full of them. Just now a glow of perfect happiness engulfed him with the heady warmth and glory of spreading sunlight across the sky after a dark storm. He even found himself short of breath with the wonder of these golden moments. His jaws nearly ached from his perpetual smile—for so long in his life an alien response. It was good, he thought, this feeling of joy. It was like stealing without the guilt.

It all so thoroughly consumed him that he scarcely saw the rendezvous camp he strolled through with Soft Wind and Grass Woman. Warning Daniel to protect the girls from unwanted advances of the carousing mountain men, Walking Feather had consented to allow the three young people the freedom and enjoyment of walking and talking their way through the camp.

Walking Feather's daughters' lack of exposure to English made little difference. Daniel had reasonable fluency in their tongue; what he lacked verbally he could make up for with universal signs.

Soft Wind and Grass Woman giggled and laughed in innocent abandon, their brown eyes sparkling as they struggled, sometimes awkward and embarrassed, with his occasional misunderstanding. Between themselves, they chattered so fast in Crow, their voices almost shrill in gaiety, that Daniel had trouble following.

As lighthearted and as lightheaded as he felt squiring the girls through the sights of rendezvous, a corner of his mind centered on the responsibility entrusted to him; Walking Feather had not granted his permission lightly.

They paused here and there to watch games of "hand," the loud and animated campfire pastime of guessing which hand held the stone or other token. Drawn by the peppering barks of gunfire, they strolled to watch the "blanket shoots" in which riflemen wagered items from their possibles in contests of marksmanship, while others wagered on the prowess of their favorite crackshots.

As preoccupied as he was in savoring his enchantment of the girls' company, Daniel was aware of the squinted and frowning envious glances of hangers-on around the campfire games and among other spectators at the shoots. In snug buckskin dresses colorful with quillwork, bleached white and downy-soft, their figures equally soft and well-formed, Soft Wind and Grass Woman were as fetching as any of the young women who strolled through the camp, most of them unattended and available.

The expressions of Walking Feather's daughters hardened as they witnessed sign language bargaining between a half-drunk trapper and a young Indian woman with the offer of trinkets or beads before strolling away together to find a secluded hideaway.

His supreme happiness undermined and his thoughts troubled at these intrusions into these charmed moments, Daniel considered that the flat area for horse racing remote from the main campground might be less unsettling or threatening.

"Shall we go to the contests of the horses?" he asked.

Her expression delighted and chattering nonstop in Crow to Grass Woman, Soft Wind impulsively caught his hand with a gentle, meaningful squeeze that sent new surges through him as she encouraged and pulled him toward the horse-race grounds. Taking the initiative, laughing happily as she did, Soft Wind grabbed for her younger sister's hand as well to pull them at a fast lope or skipping with swinging arms through the tall grass toward the horse track.

Daniel's troubled thoughts melted as the three, hand-in-hand, raced like carefree children over the broad sunlit meadow, full of breathless laughter; he wondered again when he had known such joy and freedom. Or if he ever had.

Focused on noisy wagering and shouted encouragement for a favored steed at the races, he saw no more of the hungry glances that had troubled him. A race was about to start and they found a good place at the fringe of the crowd to watch.

"The bay will win," Grass Woman proclaimed, watching with eager eyes a lively reddish-brown horse with lines that suggested Kentucky ancestry. Its opponent was a stubby gray plains mustang, strongly dappled with darker gray spots more pronounced in shoulders and rump and down the legs. It tossed its head and pawed the dirt in eagerness to run. Both were ridden by mountaineers—hunched tense in the saddle, grim and intent on the starter's gun—in grease and dirt-glazed buckskins.

"I favor the gray," Daniel called happily over the roar of the noisy bettors. "Western ponies are best at everything." Though she had dropped Grass Woman's hand after they reached the racetrack, Soft Wind still held his. Daniel wondered at its message, but happily allowed it, their fingers intertwined. He had never held anything so warm, so soft, and he made no move to resist.

"Which horse do you declare, Soft Wind?" he asked.

Her eyes came up to meet his with a depth and a meaning he couldn't understand. In an instant, merriment twinkled in them. "Both shall win," she said with a strange conviction, her words nearly drowned by the muzzle blast signal of a fired Hawken rifle. "Or," she added, "both shall lose."

In an instant, the horses had leaped to high gallop over the course that measured about a furlong, the beat of swift-pounding hoofs drumming through the ground under them and the swift-hammering thuds reaching their ears. Around them, shouted encouragement resounded in nearly every throat and rose in deafening waves over the crowded mountaineers along the route.

The two horses went by them in a blur of speed and color, neither with a distinguishing lead. They passed the finish line the same way and Daniel sensed from a distance that it would be a tough race to call.

As the riders halted and let their horses walk to calm and cool down, the official starter and referee emerged out of the crowd.

He was a short-gaited, oval-shaped man in blackened and brittle buckskins, blunt and stocky of build with a stiff, unseasoned coonskin crudely gathered and stitched with sinew for a cap, his Hawken cradled in his arms. He waddled bowlegged to the middle of the track and held up an arm for attention.

"She uz a draw, boys!" he called, his astonishingly bass voice projecting the length of the crowd. "Declared t' be a nose-to-nose finish, 'y God! All bets air off. Riders 'n hosses kin race agin t'morra mawnin' uth new wagerin' ta take place. Wun't be no more racin' t'day!"

As the crowd dispersed, Daniel grinned down at Soft Wind, whose eye level came about to his shoulders. "Soft Wind is the winner," he declared, finding himself lost in the depths of her upturned dense brown eyes.

"But not the loser," she said, her eyes searching his with a meaning undefined.

A late sun already made long shadows of cottonwoods fringing the nearby Green River tributary known as New Fork.

Grass Woman spoke up. "Shall we walk by the river before we return to my father's lodge?" she asked

Soft Wind responded by happily locking arms with the two of them and again pulling them, this time toward the tree-edged stream, with a carefree, swinging step.

They had walked a considerable distance from the activity of the rendezvous camp along the fork; with the emergence of twilight beginning to turn a sunlit land gray, they rested along the chattering stream to further enjoy its freedoms and solitude before turning back to their father's tepee at the edge of camp.

Perched on a huge stream boulder, Grass Woman, her buckskin skirt reaching mid-calf, recklessly hiked the skirt above the knees to loosen and remove her moccasins. Daniel self-consciously averted his eyes from such wanton display. But he understood Grass Woman's feelings of freedom and security with him.

"I can catch fish with my hands," she boasted, leaving Soft Wind and Daniel alone as she started gingerly tottering over the rough ground on bare feet to the stream bank. "I shall bring many for a feast this night for my mother and father. Dan-yell and Soft Wind may eat jerky." Her laughter was a gay tinkle of delight, her eyes crinkled in a smile all their own.

"So shall you, Grass Woman," Soft Wind taunted. "I have yet to see the fish you catch with your hands, little sister. Show me, and I shall catch even more for a feast for Dan-yell and me."

As Grass Woman hiked her skirts even higher to reveal brown, well-formed thighs and to avoid soaking and stretching her garment, Soft Wind again reached out to grip Daniel's hand in her inviting soft one.

"If your hands must work to hold high your skirts for all to see your beauty, Grass Woman," she called happily, "you will catch few fish! Maybe they will bite on your toes!" Soft Wind laughed happily at her sister's plight.

Grass Woman, happily knee-deep in the rushing water dancing and spangled by a waning sun, glared in mock anger from a distance at her older sister. "You wait, Soft Wind," she called, the happy chirp in her voice reaching them across the water. "You just wait!"

A crackling in the underbrush on the tangled hillside of trees and tumbled rocks above them jerked Daniel alert, jarring him with the searing flood of alarm. His startled eyes caught movement as three scruffy mountaineers about his own age emerged with menace and evil purpose out of the rustling brush.

All three wore stiff, poorly seasoned, shaped, and stitched raw deerskins. One was hatless, another with a full coyote pelt for headgear, the hide and tail dangling down his back, and the third with a battered broad-brimmed slouch hat decorated with a drooping dark brown and striped turkey feather.

Daniel rose up in alarm but protectively and wisely pushing Soft Wind behind him. In midstream, Grass Woman—eyes and mouth wide in fear—dropped her buckskin skirts to soak and swirl around her knees, her face a mask of terror.

"Well, looky here, boys. Here's the leetle squaw man with his women, just like we figured," gloated the apparent leader, the one in the coyote headgear. They were all drunk.

Daniel stood up to face the intruders, holding Soft Wind behind him. As swiftly as he opposed them, the carefree Daniel who had reveled in his happy moments with Soft Wind and Grass Woman gave way to the well-remembered and oft-rehearsed rising tide of anger and resentment boiling up to erupt and drench his soul with a bitter and mindless energy; the fevered blood of fury pounded in his temples.

"Get out!" he shrieked at the three facing and moving to flank him. His hand was mere inches from the hilt of his sheath knife.

Coyote Cap confronted him while Barehead and Turkey Feather moved evilly to his blind sides. His eyes darted, watching them. Soft Wind cowered behind him, wide-eyed and shrunken in innocent terror while Grass Woman still stood with panic-blanched features hunched and helpless in the swirling waters of New Fork.

The three leered at their find. "We figured you had more'n enough poontang to suit you, hoss, so we come on along to help you out," Coyote Cap said with a leer, a filthy lust strong in his voice.

"Wait a minute, boys," he added. "I know this here coon. Seen him a year or two back. This here's Orphan! Used to be old Skull's and that rascal Penn's pet coon and camp squaw! Worthless as a maggoty plew is this here porkeater!"

"I am Daniel England," he protested. "Leave us be." He edged closer to Soft Wind behind him as the three drew menacingly near. Daniel sensed the old remembered rising tide and trembling of insane violence building from deep within and he fought against it. He needed the strength and calm control he had watched and learned with Jacob Lyman.

"Nah, Orphan. We come along down here from ronnyvoo to have us some fun with these here squaw beauties of yours. Step aside."

Turkey Feather moved past Daniel and Soft Wind toward the stream. "I'm gettin' that one yonder there in the crick, Jack!"

"Bring her on up here, Dooley!" Coyote Cap commanded. "We-uns'll have us a go at the both of 'em!"

Grass Woman shrieked in frenzied terror to awkwardly slosh her way noisily upstream against the turgid current; screaming in panic, she struggled up the mud-bank to flee headlong into the thickets and brambles with Turkey Feather in hot, hilarious, hooting pursuit.

"C'mon here, Li'l Injun Maid!" he yelled drunkenly, only a step or two behind the hysterical Grass Woman. "Let me show you what a real man's got in his britches for ya!"

Daniel's disorganized mind was only conscious of the running and the thrashing in the woods away from him as he faced head-on the advancing, menacing Coyote Cap and Barehead.

"Just step aside, Orphan," Coyote Cap insisted, moving close. "Dooley's after the other one. Me and Luke gonna start with that leetle Injun baggage behind you. C'mon now, boy. Don't make me take my knife and spill your guts all over the woods."

Base primal and instinctive urges welled up in Daniel and he reacted. Crouching to shield the trembling Soft Wind behind him, his hands closed on a length of downed wood, a handy weapon.

Coyote Cap moved closer to stand over him in dominant menace; Daniel burst upright, swinging the thick branch underhanded from behind him with a hoarse roar of attack. He brutally brought the club up between Coyote Cap's arrogantly spread legs—with a direct hit on super-sensitive gonads. Coyote Cap, doubled over and immobile, hit the ground sideways with knees and back bent, a balled-up mass of groan and moan, hands and arms futilely groping at the agony in his crotch.

As the immobilized Coyote Cap fell away from him, Daniel rose up to face Barehead, only now beginning to back away, face frozen and beseeching, hands coming up to protest his own innocence and shield himself, his eyes wide in terror at the stormy, clenched features of the maddened man called Orphan.

Daniel's fury would not be put off. He backswung his hasty club with vicious force to slam Barehead solidly above the ear. He landed in a heap. With Soft Wind scooting back from the scene of terror and shocking violence, Daniel posed momentarily victorious over the vanquished Barehead and Coyote Cap, eyes haunted, shaking his club as if hoping they'd ask for more while the pair groveled and squirmed in pain at his feet.

Daniel's shoulders hunched and a pagan guttural rose on his lips as Daniel whipped off Coyote Cap's offensive head-gear and grasped the stinking but full hair at scalpline, the ululating call of the victor building strong and instinctive in his throat, his Green River knife nearly leaping into his grasp on its own.

Soft Wind's threat of violation would be avenged!

His Green River knife's razor edge had but scored Coyote Cap's scalpline when his bearing on the knife was abruptly stopped by the distant, invading shout of his name booming somewhere from out of forgotten depths.

"Daniel! No!" It was Jacob Lyman.

The demon within Daniel England retreated before a star-tling reality springing into his senses with Jacob's shout.

Daniel leaped away from the still stiffened and cramped body of Coyote Cap and the unconscious Barehead as Jacob raced out of the streambank thickets on a resolute sprint toward him. Daniel was further jarred with shock as his mother emerged into view a few steps behind Jacob, her face a frozen mask of disbelief.

Soft Wind was a kneeling and shrunken cocoon of fear behind Daniel, while he stood like an avenging angel over the inert Coyote Cap and Barehead, his gleaming Green River blade projecting from his fist ready and eager to count his coup with their scalps until halted by Jacob Lyman's shout.

A heavy moment of spring-tense silence was broken only by Jacob's hurrying footsteps and the soft slither-sound of the nearby stream retreating hurriedly from this scene of brutal violence. From behind Jake, Rachel approached more slowly, her face knotted with concern for what she had witnessed in her son.

Abruptly the air around them was rent by a piercing, distant scream of terror and intolerable pain of Grass Woman filling the void between the silent trees around them.

"Jacob!" Daniel yelled, leaping away from his immobile victims toward the sound, Lyman virtually at his heels.

Tracking her shout like a coondog at full cry, Daniel's fury exploded anew at the sight of the flailing bodies before him, arms and legs of Grass Woman buried and suffocating under the half-bare Dooley. His buckskin britches were bunched behind his knees, his stark white and cleaved rump savagely pumping over her with the ferocity of a steamy stallion. Around Dooley's bucking form, her Indian-bronze and bare legs flailed and kicked while her arms clawed, pulled and tugged for the release of torment.

Daniel shot a glare back at Jacob, mere steps behind him, his mentor and foster-father, his link with reality. The insistent primal call rose up stronger as with a shrill Indian cry of attack, he leaped onto the struggling bodies of white man and Indian girl. His Green River knife, still in his clutch was cocked and poised for the fatal thrust over Dooley's back.

In Daniel's extreme and bizarre confrontations with the three assailants as well as with the beast that lurked within himself, a momentary but clear vision swirled before his eyes, churned up like dust from memory dim and dark, dead and buried almost beyond recall.

He remembered the raging fire and fatigue of childhood fever and jolting wagonbed along the army caravan's road west . . . air and trail dust too hot and too thick to breathe . . . beloved mother and comforter, pulled screaming from him by brutal, strong and savage hands . . . his supreme struggle and shriek to reach out to her . . . the red-globe of full-scalped head half-seen on a sprawled body in the dust in soldier blues with dragoon second lieutenant shoulder scales . . . all around the thunder and crush and crash of massacre and the destruction of everything held as little-boy dependable and secure . . . Father. The rock-firm, father-strong protective warmth and masculine smells and feels and the child-memory defined moments of pungent sweat-strong-damp-tickle-aroma of blue uniform when little-boy was hugged, cradled, comforted and delighted by giggle-games with father at day's-end, secure smells, and feels and breathless laughter that went away, never to return and he felt looted and angry with no means to give vent to it. The horror of early-day captivity allowed the blanking of memory—only later to return with emptiness and grief.

Now, here, today, Dooley's buckskinned back between his knees shrieked out at him to avenge, repay, atone for that lost secure world and the lost eternity in a forlorn, miserable, lonely prison as captive; for father scalped and mother stolen. Abandoned, alone, unloved. These girls . . . Soft Wind . . . had restored so much. Happy, carefree, vibrant Grass Woman cruelly raped.

Already in some other deep, secret recess of his mind, only to himself, he had made his vow to one as wife and to the other as beloved sister.

The knife poised at the end of his spring-tensed arm over Dooley's back awaited only the plunge. Lyman's pounding feet raced to him. "Daniel! No!" father's voice commanded for the second time this day. It was not father's voice but it was the now-father authority—respected, admired, and loved.

In sudden obedience, Daniel tossed aside the knife. Still, in mounting inner command to avenge, he caught Dooley's wrist to impulsively thrust the arm up behind him beyond the point of endurance as the shoulder dislocated with a resounding pop of bone-joint and muscle and cartilage and howl of supreme agony.

Daniel jumped up to yank the wailing, defeated mountaineer to his feet, the wrenched arm a-dangle, the buckskin britches sinking to his ankles like huge rawhide horse hobbles, a pitiful dark and ugly knob of penis, a moment before so brutally swollen and savage, now a mere flaccid and shrunken acorn-stub peeking out of a wealth of glistening and dark curly hair.

At their feet, sprawled and sobbing, Grass Woman struggled to clutch together her destroyed white buckskin dress to cover her nakedness and her lost virtue. The dress was rudely sliced open from hem to throat by Dooley's Green River. As Daniel turned away from her ravished nakedness, he glimpsed in passing with shock and new outrage her own wedge of thick black hair perched over the spreading crimson stain of the white, once-proud buckskin garment under her from Dooley's brutal invasion and virgin rupture. Daniel's fury rode a new angry current.

He looked at Jacob, hoping father could not read his thoughts through his eyes; his new father would approve of neither the method, the madness nor the means his mind had already devised for squaring the score with the demon Dooley. Only the bastard's severed balls and scalp would satisfy.

But, Daniel knew, it could not be. Jacob would never condone it. Skull would have awarded him a jug and paraded him in camp as a hero.

Chapter Twelve

WHILE RACHEL COMFORTED THE TWO VERY FRIGHTENED Crow girls, Jake and Daniel confronted the three battered, bruised, and now thoroughly humbled attackers.

Daniel eyed his father warily; Jacob had not yet said anything about his nearly lethal behavior. At the moment, Jake had other concerns.

"They called you Jack," Lyman said to Coyote Cap, biting off his words in anger. "What's your last name?"

"Butler, sir. Jack Butler."

He looked even more angrily at Grass Woman's attacker. "From the talk, I take it your name's Will Dooley."

Dooley cradled his throbbing right arm and shoulder in his left arm, his eyes and jaws clenched in pain; Lyman offered no sympathy. Dooley only nodded painfully at Lyman in a strained gesture of assent.

"I asked you your name!" Lyman growled, his patience in short supply. "Say it, dammit!"

"Will Dooley's right." Dooley grunted his words.

Lyman's eyes swung on Barehead.

"Farmer," he said without prompting. "Lucas Farmer."

"Well, Farmer," Lyman said. "You'd've been better served to've stayed down on the farm. You all feel sick just now for getting what you had coming to you from my son there. Mark my words, you're going to feel a great deal sicker."

He studied each of them closely, thinking through his next statement.

"My son was entrusted with the safety of those girls by their father, a respected Crow warrior named Walking Feather. Now to my mind, Daniel did everything in his power to protect them. If I hadn't stopped him, he very well might have killed you all. To put it mildly, Walking Feather is going to be very unpleasant when he hears about this." His words now were ground out and emphatic. "My son will *not* take the blame for this!"

He paused again.

"We're going back to rendezvous together, all of us. You're not to say a word to anyone. I'll find my friend, Dr. Whitman. Perhaps he can give you, Butler and Farmer, something to ease your pain. Dooley, I'm sure he can set your shoulder. Then we're all going to the Indian camp for you to explain and apologize to Walking Feather."

Butler spoke up. "You'd take a Injun's side agin yer own kind, sir?"

Lyman's face froze in sudden fury and his arm came up as if to backhand Butler in the face. Stopping himself in mid-motion, he looked across the small clearing at Rachel, almost in apology for his angry, impulsive behavior. His wife crouched with a mothering arm around each of the still-trembling girls.

"You are not my kind, Butler, in any way, shape or form! And you three have the gall to call yourselves mountain men! You bring shame to our trade. So mind your tongue, Butler. When I need you to speak up, I'll ask. As a matter of fact, I intend to turn you over to Walking Feather after you've explained and cleared my son's name with him. I don't think you need to worry that he'll burn you at the stake or skin you alive. He may make you wish, though, that you'd thought of something else for excitement this evenin'.

"Again, you will speak to no one until we've seen Walking Feather. The less said of the disgrace and pain you've brought this young girl, the better. What Walking Feather wants told of it is up to him. Now I've spoken my piece, we'll be on our way."

"Don't turn us over to that Injun, Mr. Lyman, please!" Farmer pleaded.

Lyman's darted look was totally barren of sympathy. "You should've thought about the consequences before you came charging in here, Farmer!"

RACHEL HAD BROUGHT a blanket for their lovers' tryst, and it came in handy to cover Grass Woman for the walk back to rendezvous.

Their first stop was at Dr. Whitman's lodge to have the injured examined. Leaving Daniel to guard their prisoners and Rachel comforting the girls, Lyman found Rev. Parker and Dr. Whitman in the lodge deeply involved in Bible study and discussion. When Jake briefly explained the nature of his call, Rev. Parker courteously remembered other duties, and left the two men alone.

Jake came out minutes later to ask Rachel to take Grass Woman in to see Dr. Whitman; Rachel, who also knew much of the Crow tongue from her captivity with the Cheyenne, patiently convinced the distraught young woman that while Dr. Whitman was a white medicine man, it would be good for her to have his advice on her injuries. Looking at the loving, caring Rachel with grateful, trusting eyes, Grass Woman consented.

Inside his lodge, the doctor only found it necessary to discuss the attack and her injuries with Grass Woman briefly, with Rachel interpreting. He decided not to subject her to the embarrassment of a physical examination.

"The hemorrhage," he explained to Rachel, "is not pleasant nor painless, but is a natural consequence of such a brutal attack on a virgin. She's young, healthy, and strong. She needs to be taken home, cleaned up, rested, and fed.

Most of the harm, Rachel, is to her mind. But that won't be permanent. To weather it, she'll need love and care and understanding in these first days. All of which I know you and Jake and Daniel and her family will provide in abundant quantity. That's the best medical advice I can give."

Dr. Whitman smiled benevolently at the two women. "Now, I'd better see to Jake and Daniel's victims. Sounds like they are worse off than this plucky young woman!"

Rachel saw Grass Woman observing Dr. Whitman's smile with a puzzled look.

"The white medicine man," she explained to Grass Woman in Crow, "thinks Grass Woman is very brave and very strong, and feels very badly for what has happened to you. He says he is sure you will feel all right very soon."

Grass Woman's large brown eyes beamed in gratitude on Dr. Whitman.

AT WALKING FEATHER'S lodge, Lyman called out his old friend for a talk while Rachel took Soft Wind and Grass Woman inside to their mother. Walking Feather only glanced at the girls' faces and at their disheveled condition in passing, noting that his youngest daughter was shrouded in a blanket. Reading the sign, his eyes narrowing in a father's justifiable outrage at the five white men waiting for him outside, his first words were directed at Daniel and at Jake Lyman.

"I do not have to ask what has happened to my youngest daughter. A father can read truth and pain in his child's eyes," he said, speaking mainly to Jake Lyman. He turned on Daniel with a vicious look. "I trusted you and you betrayed me!"

Walking Feather's flinty eyes swung angrily on Butler, Farmer and Dooley standing with heads down a few steps away.

"Are these the young men you sold my daughters to?" he demanded of Daniel.

Jake Lyman spoke up for his stepson, moving close to Walking Feather to face him. "There was no betrayal, no blame on Daniel's part, Walking Feather! You must not think ill of him. These three will tell you what happened and it will vindicate Daniel."

"He gave me his word, Jacob! That is betrayal. He returns my lovely children to my lodge dirtied in their minds and their bodies by these demons who dare to call themselves men."

"Had I not been there to command him to put down the knife, Walking Feather, Daniel would now be here to hand you their scalps. In defending your daughters, he was as brave a warrior as I have seen."

Walking Feather studied the three sorry-looking wretches. One had an ugly, purple swelling behind his ear, another with an injured arm carried useless in Dr. Whitman's cloth sling. The third was hunched as if in lingering pain.

Lyman smiled at Walking Feather. "The one with the coyote hat was struck in a man's most sensitive place. Daniel disabled him with the skill of a mighty warrior. It was wondrous to see."

Walking Feather looked at the still slightly-bent Butler, and then at the others, a knowing grin growing on his face. "Such lessons are better than losing one's scalp. Such shame may make men of them after all. But from the look of those three, I think not. They will live their lives making such foolish mistakes over and over and not learning. Daniel has my forgiveness. To count coup on three enemies without himself being wounded marks Daniel as a great warrior."

Daniel studied Walking Feather's features proudly but intently, knowing a decision expressed by Walking Feather stood for all time.

"What of these three?" Jake asked. "My son Daniel and I have brought them to Walking Feather to decide punishment for the disgrace they have brought upon his lodge."

Walking Feather looked at him quizzically. "Jacob brings his white brothers to me, a Crow, that I may judge their fate?"

"These are not my brothers simply because their skin is white any more than Walking Feather thinks of the Crows' ancestral enemies, the Sioux, as brothers. In the mind of Jacob and of his son, Daniel, Walking Feather's lodge has been shamed by these men. It is right and just that Walking Feather should make the judgment."

Butler, Dooley, and Farmer watched Walking Feather in keen and fearful apprehension.

Walking Feather pounded the heel of his extended right hand smartly into the upended palm of his left in the sign of decision.

"Walking Feather speaks," he declared. "Walking Feather releases these men to the guilt and the shame that shall live forever in their hearts. And to the foolish mistakes they will make again and again in their lives. Perhaps soon enough they will repay such foolishness with their scalps. The word shall pass of their evil deeds, here and now these days at the white man's rendezvous, and in the moons to come that they may be banished by their honorable white brothers."

Lyman turned to Butler, Farmer, and Dooley. "I don't suppose you boys ever cared enough to have learned a little of the Crow tongue to understand what Walking Feather has decreed. You're very lucky. He's lettin' you off without any sort of real punishment. You've saved your scalps for now. He's lettin' you go."

"Sounds like he's going to spread the word, Mr. Lyman. You said he prob'ly wouldn't," Butler protested.

"I said it was up to him. As I understand him, the word'll go out against you at this rendezvous. You'll be best served to skedaddle first whack."

Walking Feather held up his hand to stop Lyman.

"Walking Feather is not finished," he continued, the edge of anger still sharp in his voice. "I will know the scalps of these three men if I see them. Little escapes my eye in knowing these men again. Or telling of them to others of their foul deeds. After one sleep they must be gone from this white man's rendezvous and after the Moon of Falling Leaves must be gone from the country west of the Platte and the Missouri. I shall send the word to my brothers and to my enemies that I will pay many horses for these scalps if they are seen in these places ever again!"

Lyman again interpreted. "In case you missed his words, Walking Feather directs that you pack your possibles and settle your affairs here and be on your way east by tomorrow's sunset. Get east of the Platte before the snows. If you are found in this country after that—or ever—he will pay dearly in horses for your scalps. It will be a rich bounty for the warrior or trapper who sees you. And the word will be passed, as far and wide as Walking Feather can. And Daniel and I will help spread the word. You'll be well served to heed the warning."

"Hey," Butler piped up. "He cain't do that. This here's a free kentry!"

"It was until you boys got to feelin' your oats with Daniel and Walking Feather's daughters this evenin'," Lyman said, his voice again a growl. "You'd best skedaddle before he changes his mind."

Lyman looked at Walking Feather who nodded in understanding and agreement.

"Do something right for a change," Lyman commanded. "Git!"

The three looked at one another sheepishly and walked quickly away toward the main rendezvous camp.

Chapter Thirteen

JAKE LYMAN PICKED UP A SMALL ROCK AND IDLY TOSSED IT TO thunk into the streamside swirls and eddies at their feet, Marcus Whitman, readying his belongings for the return trip east with Broken Hand Fitzpatrick's mule wagons, took time out for a walk with Jake down along the river.

The gentility of stream and sun-warmed air inclined them toward deep discussion.

"Something's caused me to wonder, Jake," Whitman said. "Your stepson valorously fought off those three toughs to protect the Indian girls. Shows uncommon courage. But, I'm curious. When I examined young Butler, I noticed a distinct knife cut at the hairline, not a serious incision, but certainly a noticeable scoring or tracing of the surface skin, the obvious and intentional work of a knife."

Lyman chuckled grimly. "Odd you should have noticed, Mark," he said, feeling close and trusting with Whitman. "The three of us, Daniel, Rachel, and myself, have finally come out in the open and talked after skirting around the subject for months now. We're all relieved, I think."

"Translation please, Jake."

"Daniel's five years in Indian captivity. There was also a time of virtual darky-like servitude when he was treated shabbily and gravely influenced by a man named Skull, a nondescript frontier rogue, a booze-ridden killer-animal best described as fiendish and evil from the top of his bald head to the tips of his toes. That Rachel and I are able to salvage anything in Daniel after his exposure to such evil is the true cause for wonder."

"I begin to see. In the attack yesterday, Daniel's demon behavior emerged. With Butler immobilized, Daniel was about to scalp him when, I presume, you somehow intervened."

"I guess you see things with a third eye, Mark. It was a lucky coincidence. Rachel and I were out for a walk by the river. We found the three—Butler, Farmer, and Dooley—dead-drunk and ready to kill Daniel if necessary to have their way with the girls."

"Do you see why I despise the use of spirits, Jake?"

"I hope you won't hold it against me, Mark, but I do take an occasional drink. But I hold in the lowest contempt any man who does not know his limits."

"If all topers were like you, Jake, I'd find little to criticize. I suppose my problem is with the weak-willed in general."

"Daniel isn't. Weak-willed. He has a lot of bitterness yet about those lost years. He's made a great deal of progress since coming under his mother's influence again. Only now and again have I seen that anger in his eyes and the viciousness in words and actions that I knew when I first rescued him. Most times he's about as agreeable and likable as you'll find in a young man his age."

"He's on the road to healing, Jake," Whitman reassured.

"His behavior yesterday has shaken my faith, Mark. Indeed, he did inflict that knife cut on Butler's forehead. He was ready to scalp, and not just the topknot. The whole head! What scares me is that that's the way he saw his father scalped. Something evil is buried in him, Mark, and buried deep. I arrived in time to stop him.

"Then when we heard Grass Woman's screams, he raced ahead of me to where she was being attacked and leaped on top of Dooley. He had the knife raised for the stab when I shouted at him and again he stopped."

"Hard to say, Jake. Hard to say. I can probe for bullets, and I can suture wounds. I set broken bones, and I can usually figure on medicine and treatment to ease the pain and the fevers of the sick. Warped and unacceptable behavior in normally level and placid people—such as Daniel—I neither understand nor have answers for. I feel so helpless in such situations. As I do now—for your sake, and Rachel's."

For a long moment, Whitman studied Jake Lyman's face.

"I can offer two prescriptions, Jake," he said finally. "The first from a doctor with an intense Christian upbringing. That is in faith and a strong belief in God's love and mercy. We've never discussed where you stand on the subject, nor do I think it's necessary now. But were I to offer a course of healing for Daniel's, it would begin with asking God's help.

"My second prescription is equally easy to administer. Humans—and even animals—respond admirably to its magical healing powers. You and Rachel have already started."

Lyman studied Whitman quizzically. Whitman responded to the look with an understanding smile.

"It's a word some men are not comfortable with, Jake. I'm sure where Rachel is concerned you are. Those three bullies yesterday could benefit greatly from its healing powers. The magical word, Jake, is *love*.

"The word is often misunderstood because it has so many meanings. In yours and Rachel's caring ways with Daniel, you show your love every day. That's why I said that despite his dangerous behavior yesterday, he is on the road to healing. He'll bear watching but, again Jake, I believe Daniel will justify your faith in his ultimate goodness."

Jake Lyman sensed profound relief. "You're amazing, Mark. You make so much sense. You so easily cut right to the heart of things."

Whitman grinned again. "Not amazing, Jake. Maybe I've looked at life from a slightly different perspective, that's all. As a Christian and a man of healing. If you'd really thought it through, I'm sure you'd have reached the same conclusions."

Lyman grunted. "I doubt it."

"Don't sell yourself short, Jake Lyman."

"I try not to."

"There's another phase of the treatment that should hasten recovery."

"What's that?"

"It's physical. Rachel can demonstrate it in her mother's embraces and caring touches. You can show it in a firm handshake or a fatherly arm around Daniel's shoulder. Such simple things pay vast dividends. Find more opportunities to show your love."

Another long silence grew between them. "I'll hate to see you go, Mark."

"And I wish you could come back with me and stand up for me at my wedding with Narcissa, as you asked me to do for you. This time next year she'll be here with me."

"I'm honored, Mark. Deeply honored. I'd have to be gone most of a year. I'd miss the fall trapping, and I couldn't come back in winter. By the time I got back after the thaws, the spring hunt would be about over and the prime would be off the beaver."

"I know." Whitman said wistfully.

"I have an idea, Mark. Why not get married out here, like we did! From what you say, there'll be a proper minister or two in your company next year."

"Nice thought, Jake, but the Board of Foreign Missions that supports these missionary ventures wouldn't look with favor on our travel together unmarried."

"There's always a catch in life, isn't there?"

"So much to plan, so much depending on events and works and things accomplished or assembled in proper order and on schedule. Narcissa and her parents look toward a date in mid-February next year for the knot-tying. We start west as soon as the roads and the rivers open with the thaw."

"We'll celebrate with you next summer at rendezvous."

"Narcissa and I will look forward to that."

"I suppose I should temper that with if I'm here. If there's even a rendezvous."

"Why the doubt, Jake?"

"Hard to explain. Change. Everything's changing. Beaver nearly trapped out and that's a worry. Value of the plews dropping, cost of trade goods going sky-high. They're starting to make dress hats out of silk from China. In England and on the continent, felt's being made from other, cheaper animal fibers. This way of life is seriously threatened."

"That sounds to me like nothing more than good healthy competition. What can be wrong with that? It's a call for some creative thinking and industry on your part."

Lyman felt uncomfortable with Whitman's carefree optimism; the man simply did not understand the problem. "Ordinarily, I'd agree," he said. "But that's not all. Indians more and more being treated shabbily and abused by the traders and the government. They're pushing whiskey at them to confuse them and then to rob them. White men coming in are pushier, more greedy. Getting nasty. This incident yesterday with Walking Feather's daughters is a good—well, not so good—example. The Indians are growing less tolerant of whites. And that may be putting it mildly."

"I'm a greenhorn out here. I have absolutely no right to pass judgment. Or even to make observations. But also as you know, there's another side to my being here. After a great deal of study and soul-searching, I've dedicated my life to bringing the best of American and Christian principles to those Indians in the Oregon country."

"I hope you'll understand, Mark, that I'm not real envious. That's a mighty tall order. An uphill fight."

"I've no doubt about the nature of my undertaking. It's not been entered into lightly. Narcissa's also aware of the hardships and the dangers. We've read a great deal about the Western Indian situation from reliable, objective sources. I'm also aware of the extreme views, and the sorts of things I can expect to cope with from the extremists in Indian affairs. So I'm pretty well grounded in what I'm up against. To my way of thinking, a sensible approach leavened with understanding—and that word I just used with you, love—ought to accomplish something in the name of goodness and decency. It must begin on a small scale, even if it begins with me."

"You're an intelligent man, devout and dedicated, Mark. If anyone can make sense and progress out of this sometimes hopeless situation, it's you."

"You know, Jake, in some of the extremist writers about the proposed handling of these Western Indians, I hear the words 'white superiority' ringing in the lines and between the lines. This will come as a surprise to you, but I've arrived at a sense that I am—as a white man—superior."

Lyman saw an almost mischievous grin flit across Whitman's face.

"You'll have to explain that one, Mark."

"We, some of us—and I count you in the flock—are the masters."

"I fail to understand."

"We are, my good friend, masters *of the means*—applied judiciously and with love—to bring greater fulfillment and the sweet sense of peace to these native people without totally disrupting a lifestyle that already carries with it a high degree of serenity. We must never lose sight of that delicate balance. But, as you say with the trapper's life, change—disruptive change—is in the wind. Unfortunately, it is an ill wind. It will be even more devastating for the Indian, unless they are prepared well ahead to make the necessary adjustments in their ways and in their thinking. It can't happen overnight. Rome wasn't built in a day, and all that. Now's the time to take the necessary steps to prepare them for what's ahead. Before it's too late. To gird them with the knowledge and the strength to assimilate and adjust to change. Otherwise—and harken to my words, Jake—they will be rolled over and crushed to near oblivion. The juggernaut of Yankee imperialism is unstoppable! Even the stern courage of the great Indian warriors will not quench it."

The power and the might of Whitman's words had taken Lyman's breath away. "I suppose I've thought that, Mark, but never could put it into words that way you just have."

"But don't you disagree?"

"Never! Again, Mark, you cut straight to the heart of the matter."

Whitman chuckled, his expression brightening and lightening after his serious dialogue. "Hew to the line, no matter in whose face the chips may fly!"

"By contrast to imperialism, good old Yankee wisdom," Lyman observed dryly, but with a smile. "We both heard it at grandfather's knee."

"And it is Old Testament wisdom of the Psalmists that God grants us three score years and ten of strength—which I interpret as opportunities, each day a blessed opportunity— to make a difference in this life, in this world. Seventy times 365, Jake! Can you conceive it?! My feeble ciphering fails me. But I intend to use what days of the years, or fraction thereof that God may grant me, to find and pursue *the means* to benefit mankind in the striving for a more perfect world. My faith demands it!"

Lyman shook his head. "Why do I think I'm listening to sermon, Mark? Seriously, you continue to give me things to think about, and to regret your leaving. My life could stand many more chances to stroll by mountain streams to talk with someone of your dedication and strength of character."

"Next year. Same time, same place, my good friend."

"A year is a long time."

"So why not spend it productively? Creatively?"

"I intend to."

"Trapping, of course. Earning the means to survive and prosper. To bring love and fulfillment to Rachel, and sensible adjustments to a new, bewildering world to Daniel. Worthy endeavors. Surely enough to challenge a man."

"I'd say so."

"But is it really enough, Jake?"

"Why not?"

"Walking Feather, for one. Your friend. Is it enough that he's been provoked to banish, on the fear of death and mutilation, the three monsters who brutalized and terrorized his beautiful daughters? How will this Crow Indian you so respect and admire fare in the face of this humiliation and disruption of his home and family? Don't you, who cherishes the same land and the same passions as he, owe him something? You've told me that Daniel has shown a fondness for Soft Wind, but that his potentially violent behavior could cloud his role as a mature husband—if it comes to that."

"All good points, Mark, I'll grant you. Food for thought. I owe Walking Feather a great deal. I've not lost sight of that."

"You still miss the overriding imperative, Mr. Lyman."

Jake began to feel uncomfortable under the light of having his inner self so closely examined by a man of such intensities as Marcus Whitman. "You lead me into some kind of trap of words, Mark. Imperialism, imperatives. What's it all mean?"

"No trap at all, Jake. I'll be back in a year with a young, eastern-bred wife who I hope will be strong enough to endure the hostile wilderness of the Columbia River country and to expand our healing influence and to educate. We'll bring with us several missionaries equally unprepared for the rigors and hostilities of the country as well as of its native inhabitants."

"My roots and my work are here, several hundred miles from where you propose to build your base. Still, I'll do everything I can to help you."

Whitman studied Jake intently. "I've thought of this deeply. Would you listen to some suggestions, Jake?"

"Haven't I so far?"

"Granted. Again I may speak from an altogether naive viewpoint. You respect these Indians, those who are your friends, such as Walking Feather. They, in turn, respect you, and will listen to you. Become a missionary, Jake!"

Jake belted out an astonished guffaw. "Hah! I'd be miserable either at preaching a sermon or tending to the sick and injured!"

"I don't mean anything of the kind, either. I suppose I mean establishing closer bonds with the Indians, sharing the best of our methods with them, those that may be acceptable and adaptable to them. Building alliances and confidence rather than distance and distrust. Learning more of their ways and adapting or adopting them to improve the quality of life of our people out here."

"Many of us already do that."

"Then what a marvelous base you have to build on! Develop a council. Something small and informal. Don't threaten their natural chain of leadership. Remember the delicate balance. Begin with you and Walking Feather. Remember you work to counteract the evil in the white invasion and to build on its goodness. Forgive my talk of lofty ideals, but that, Jake, is the shining star you must reach for and strive for."

Jake sensed new zest and inspiration with Whitman's words.

"Keep it simple; a loose-knit working operation. Your friendship with Walking Feather should help it. Rachel and Daniel, as former captives, must be familiar with Indian attitudes and philosophies. Turn that negative experience into a force for good. Begin small and grow slowly. But grow! Look at what Jesus has accomplished worldwide with but twelve apostles."

"That's hardly a fair comparison, Mark."

"Granted. But a good model. One more point, Jake, and then I must get back. You tell me of the depletion of the beaver while the price of the pelts also falls. It makes sense, then, that the way to keep up with the changes is to produce more beaver."

"But the streams are being trapped out."

"It sounds ridiculous and unworkable, but one of the first steps for your trapper-Indian council could be to set aside areas, streams, as zones of conservation. Enforce a trapping ban for a year in these streams to allow the beaver population to multiply. Then, those that have been opened to trapping can be closed and allowed to regenerate the next year. Start small. Just within your close trapper friends and Walking Feather's Indian neighbors. Some of them could enforce the trapping ban as wardens or stewards; not as police. Stress peaceful, persuasive means—not violence. The idea might grow. If everyone could be convinced of the potential bene-fits, it could work. With the beaver as with the Indians, as ye sow so shall ye reap."

"Sounds good on the face of it, sitting here by this stream, Mark. Making it work is quite another thing. They've already got enough restrictions on their freedoms. Sounds like more government than it's worth."

"Then I have one final question, Jacob Lyman. Remember that you are a *master of the means* to a better life for these Western Indians. As such, your lifestyle in these mountains? . . . What is it *worth*? To them—and to you?"

1836

Chapter Fourteen

THE SALOON SMELLED OF FOUL KEEP AND WAS AS GRAY AND uninspiring as a dank day of heavy overcast.

The dismal odor of the place was a depressing blend of old puke, dried mud, and soft shit tracked in and ground up underfoot. This disgusting dust sat atop everything, or was swept up into the air with a mildewed bar rag and occasionally swamped out with a damp and musty rag-mop wielded with tired indifference. Such poor housekeeping extended to the sharp assaulting stench of the goboons—rarely-tended, sawdust-filled plug tobacco boxes for the more fastidious spitters—as they wafted their vile incense into the atmosphere along with the clinging remembrance of layers of old tobacco smoke. The rank odors of cheap, hastily-stilled whiskey hovered over and tainted the fringes of the other unsavory aromas.

Lighting, when it was needed after dark, came from a motley, dim, and scanty assortment of lanterns—not lamps—secured to the square-hewn rafter beams or stout upright supports. In daylight, operators of the barn-like structure hoped that the wan light through an open door and one small mullioned window beside it—opaque from neglect and age—would be sufficient; still it was dark enough along the bar or at the drinking tables in any kind of light for one to miss a dead fly or a roach in a glass of whiskey.

123

A man came into such a St. Louis dive, one of many dotting the Mississippi's riverfront, to drink himself into oblivion and little else. It was a far cry from sociable settings for cultured drinkers. Bloody and brutal brawling with the occasional crippling or fatal knifing were common but secondary to the large gray hall's primary function as a place to take on a cargo and get drunk, night-before or morning-after. So, what mattered if a man began his day sprawled cold, cramped, and remorseful with the collywobbles, miserable and penitent in a bleak alley, cheap hotel, or under a pile of leaves in the woods. The vague and stumbling, bleary-eyed and trembling, pain-roaring memory would first stimulate a resolution to never let the demon in again! Such resolve, however, was fleeting. It was a new day and the hair of the dog would clear the cobwebs and ease the pain. Forget the shakes; go get a jug! After a while in the light-headed euphoria of a fresh drunk, a man even forgot the rotten stink of the place.

The prevailing philosophy of its clientele—this morning limited to three miserable looking young men in tattered buckskins—seemed to be "what's the use of gettin' sober when you're gonna get drunk all over again!"

In a dark, recessed corner of this early morning hell on earth, with their heads together but speaking little, huddled over a rejuvenating jug, the jittery stomachs of Jack Butler, Will Dooley, and Luke Farmer were still swollen with charred, dried and hardened venison hastily broiled over a too-hot fire in the outlying woods after a lucky, early dawn shot. The buck's carcass, apart from choice portions for their breakfast, was abandoned. They turned in the raw hide at a riverfront tannery for the price of the half-filled jug that now allowed the sweet dream of peace to return.

At the end of the bar across the room from them, the barkeep dozed on a tall stool.

Movement—a shadow crossing the open doorway—brought their heads up. The spread-legged silhouette of a man surveyed the place from the threshold; even at the distance and undefined against the backlighting from the street, he brought with him a sinister tightness to the air.

As they watched, the whip-thin stranger began an easy, rangy amble toward the bar, his back ramrod straight and shoulders squared. Now in the dim light, it could be seen that his hatless head was as devoid of hair as an egg. His eyes were large and dark orbs in a face that seemed to have the skin stretched over it. His thin, tight lips were perpetually drawn back from well-set teeth, giving him the death's-head appearance that gave him the only name anyone ever knew.

Jack Butler uttered it softly in the wake of an astonished gasp.

"Skull!"

"You sure?" Farmer asked.

"Sure as hell!" Will Dooley whispered. "I seen him just the once at Fort Union with Thomas Penn and that Lyman kid they used to call Orphan that landed us in the shit at ronnyvoo last season. That's Skull sure as hell!"

"Heard Skull went to jail out east somewhere," Butler added. "Some trouble that son-a-bitch Lyman got him into."

Skull had stopped midway in the long bar; the barkeep watched him impassively from his perch on the high stool behind the bar.

Skull reached into baggy pants, which looked like hand-me-downs several times removed, and tossed some silver on the bar; he turned his head slowly to icily regard the lounging bartender. Skull's words were angry and clipped.

"What the hell does it take to get a drink in this place?"

The bartender eased off the stool and ambled toward where Skull stood watching him. "You only got to ask, Baldy," he growled loudly, pulling a whiskey jug off the counter behind the bar and reaching under it for a glass from a stack of tumblers that were hazy and chipped from extensive use. He ambled up to Skull.

"How you want it, for chrissake? You want a glass of whiskey or do you want I leave the jug?"

"Leave it," Skull said, his voice low and level.

The bartender thumped down the jug and the frosty-scoured glass. "That'll be six bits." He made a reach for some of the silver.

Like a striking snake, Skull's right hand darted out to clamp a vise-like grip on the bartender's extended wrist. He twisted the wrist to bring a howl of pain from the barkeep and banged the man's elbow brutally on the bar. The barkeep bent forward in pain, bringing his nose within inches of Skull's.

"Jesus!" the agonized barkeep howled hoarsely. "Come on!"

Skull twisted the tortured arm even more until the barkeep stood on tiptoes to lean over the bar toward him for relief.

"Next time you call me Baldy," Skull snarled into the man's face, "I'll do the same thing to your goddam neck and you'll be servin' this swill to the Devil amongst the spitfires down below! Take your goddam six bits and go on back and siddown."

The bartender, his face ashen and frozen in pain, awkwardly picked up coins with his left hand and, gingerly holding his injured elbow, limped bent-over in pain back toward his stool.

Skull lifted the jug and filled the glass with the amber whiskey; it had the capacity of a small cup. With one swig, he downed half the contents, took a breath and tossed off the second half.

He filled the glass again and turned back to the room, nonchalantly resting his back and one elbow on the bar, holding the glass in front of him now for sipping. His eyes took in the three watching him. He touched the rim of the glass to his forehead in a sort of jaunty salute.

"Mornin', boys," he called pleasantly. They saw that in addition to being bald, Skull had neither eyebrows nor eyelashes. It was well-known among mountain men that for some reason lost in the mists of time, Skull no longer had the ability to raise hair.

It was also quipped around the campfires, however, that Skull's skinning knife had raised a veritable forest of hair. Skull was well known as a killer deluxe.

"Mr. Skull," Jack Butler called in acknowledgment. "Can we buy you a drink?"

Skull took one more look at the bartender hunched on his stool preoccupied with favoring his aching arm. Almost on impulse, Skull caught up his jug from the bar on his index finger and in a loose-jointed, characteristic gait of men at his degree of brutal arrogance, made his jaunty way across the saloon floor to where Dooley, Farmer, and Butler sat watching and waiting.

His erect, almost military, bearing belied his reputation as a sneak killer and backshooter.

His clothing, however, was another matter. Skull's shirt had fared no better than his pants and over it was a badly worn brown and thick wool coat a size or two too small.

The seated trio also saw that Skull wore common farmer's brogans; the leather upper of one shoe had turned crisp and parted from the sole to expose a row of unsocked toes. Butler, Farmer, and Dooley looked at one another in bewilderment.

His hands occupied with glass and jug, Skull skillfully hooked a foot around a nearby chair to edge it up to an empty place at their table.

He thumped his jug and glass down and settled into the chair, looking them over with a keen eye.

"Obliged for the hospitality, boys," he said his death's-head grin beamed on them. "As you see from the ways of yon barkeep, it's a rare commodity in these parts."

Jack Butler cocked his head in assent while the others simply studied Skull in awe; among the lower lifes in the western mountain trade, the legend named Skull had the renown of a lesser god. He was probably ten years older than they.

Butler again took the initiative. "Butler's the name, Skull. Jack Butler. This here's Will Dooley and yonder is Lucas, er, Luke . . . Farmer."

"Here's my jug," Skull said. "I'm buyin' the first one."

The three filled their glasses and saluted Skull with them before drinking.

"Them buckskins. You ain't St. Louis boys. Mountain boys, I'm bettin'. High Missouri country. I don't know you, ain't seen you before, but you got the look of trappers. The spring trapping is still going on. You're back down awful early."

Butler looked at Dooley and Farmer cautioning them with his eyes to let him do the talking.

"We, uh, decided to come east after ronnyvoo last fall," he explained.

"Did that well, eh?"

"We did all right," he lied. "We heard you went to prison, Skull."

Skull grinned, and there was a gloating in his eyes. "I don't mind tellin' you. They'll have a tough time gettin' old Skull back in there again. Yeah, they put me away for thirty years on the trumped-up charges of Alexander MacLaren of the Western Fur Company and a puppet son-a-bitch he bought and paid for by the name of Lyman. Saying Thomas Penn and I were out to wreck the Western Fur Company."

"We know Lyman. How come you're not in prison?"

Skull grinned again. "I imagine there's a pretty high price tag on my head right now back there in New York State. But I know you boys wouldn't turn me in. I'd just get out again and come after you and give you what those prison guards got."

Butler watched Skull almost coldly, while Dooley and Farmer had eyes as big as bowls. "What'd you do?" Dooley asked.

"Just plain lucky. Found a nice long piece of stout wire like out of a piano. Don't know where it came from. But there it was. I fastened little wood handles on each end.

Could pretty much hide it from the prison guards in my armpit or wrapped around my leg. When my chance came, I like to taken that guard's head plumb off. Blood spouted clear to the ceilin' like some of them hot fountains in Colter's Hell out on the Yellowstone. I taken his hoss pistol and shot the next guard. Then, bango!, I was out o' there in the open runnin' west! Just plain lucky. Headed on out to the Shinin' Mountains again. Square the score with Lyman—lift a little of his hair for good measure—and get my orphan boy back!"

"How'd you get all the way to St. Louis?" Farmer asked, a rapt expression in his unblinking eyes.

Skull splashed his tumbler full again from his jug and had a long sip. His normally tense posture relaxed; he was beginning to feel the green St. Louis whiskey and turning talkative.

"T'wan't easy! I come out of there in them prison stripers, white canvas clothes with black bands painted all around that a man can see for five miles. The prison never gave a man nothing between his hide and them stiff canvas stripers. Lived, worked, ate, and slept in the damn things. Coarse as tree bark, them son-a-bitching stripers was. Raked the hide right off a man! Yes, sir. Even a funny little hat they gave me that I couldn't keep on his ball head of mine. Drove me nuts trying to keep that damned thing on and them yellin' at me to keep it there!"

Skull seemed to delight in the warmth of the whiskey and of the admiring limelight focused on him by three porkeater boys. Their jug now made the rounds. Skull wisely saved his.

"Yes, sir, by God! Traveled by night—had to in them stripers—no food for three days. Even longer than that before I found me a drink of whiskey. These here duds come off a hardpan farmer there in New York State. He wa'n't too charitable about my needs. I had thet old hoss pistol, boys, and that scared him, but in my haste I hadn't secured the guard's powder an' ball. So, that farmer and me had a set-to with my old piano wire and his neck. Like with that guard, I painted up his parlor juicy red, I'm here to tell you, and his wife set up a caterwaulin' such as you never heard."

Skull again filled his glass from their jug and half-emptied it in one swig.

"I hauled the old woman out to the stable and chained 'er down proper. She had pork chops and fried spuds in a skillet on the stove and biscuits in the oven, all done to a turn for their breakfast, so I had my first good meal in I don't know when. Damned if that old cuss didn't have him a whiskey jug put by. And I found it. My first drink in what? A year? Maybe more. It just ain't Christian, boys, what I had to put up with in court and in that New York State prison because of that son-a-bitch Lyman!"

Skull emptied his glass and reached for their jug again.

"I saved the best to last to tell you boys. That man had a bodacious beautiful daughter, sixteen maybe. Hair the color of fall straw. She was dartin' around the house tryin' to get out a door and me runnin' happy with the jug cuttin' 'er off an' tryin' to keep 'er herded in like runnin' buffler off a cliff drop."

Skull chuckled, remembering, and studied them with bleary eyes; they were better off than he was. His lifelong affinity for the hootch had been interrupted for almost a year and a half; in rare consideration, Butler, Farmer, and Dooley understood, and gave Skull plenty of room to be himself.

"I'll remember that chil' and our shinin' times till my dyin' day. Her screechin' and clawin' riled me up proper for choice doin's. I taken her down on the softest goose-down comforter ever on her mama's old four-poster. Boys, it was like shovin' your stiffy in a virgin angel on a heavenly cloud. First time I had a woman in a pair of years and sweet as honey. Them was prime doin's, them was!"

Skull paused again for a swig of whiskey.

"I found his money cache and I taken stuff I could barter with down the way and a good hoss and headed for the river and the first boat. That was maybe four weeks ago. Gonna find some money in St. Louis to get outfitted again and get back up there to square things with that son-a-bitch Lyman. Somebody'll sure want to catch me for the bounty and put me back in the *calaboose* in New York State, so I figure doin' more than my regular share of fightin' and killin'. When you boys goin' back?"

Butler had had enough to drink to make him frank. "We can't."

"What do you mean you can't?"

"They put us out. Lyman and his Injun friend. We figured to have some fun with a couple of leetle squaws Orphan had took down along the river. He lodgepoled me in the nuts and Farmer upside the head. Orphan was about to lift my ha'r till Lyman and his woman showed up. He'd even started the cut . . ."

Butler pulled his hair back from his forehead to show Skull the small, thin, and white scar.

Skull coughed out a guffaw. "By God, I learnt that boy good, I did!"

"Lyman made him stop afore he started skinnin'. It was that close! Then Orphan heard old Dooley here climbin' up on one of them leetle squaws and run over there and was about to backstab him when Lyman yelled at him again to quit! Else you'd be just be a-palaverin' with two of us this mawnin'."

Skull looked at Dooley. "You're mightily lucky."

"Lyman and the boy—they own up they is father and son now—taken us to them leetle squaws' pappy. Damn Injun lovers! They warned us we wouldn't get hurt if we'd get east of the Platte and never come back. Else this Crow name of Walkin' Feather has posted a passel of ponies to the man what brings in our skulps."

Skull's hairless, shrunk-skin face had an incredulous look. "That's keepin' you boys in St. Louis?!"

"What would you do?"

"Hells fire! I was born with a price on my head. You stay up there and fight! No man orders me around ner drives me off! You can't turn around up in that country there without somebody's after your scalp. And you let Lyman and some pipsqueak Indian scare you home to mama! You boys has got a lot to learn."

Butler looked sheepishly at Farmer and Dooley.

"Somethin' else you'd like to know, Skull. Word is that Lyman's in cahoots with the Injuns real thick since ronny-voo. Got councils o' trappers an' Injuns sittin' around talkin' an' helpin' one another. Got streams now they won't let nobody trap so's the beaver grow up more leetle beavers. Lyman's fixin' to take over that kentry for hisself. Him and that Dr. Whitman!"

"That sounds like something Lyman would fix up. We can figure ways to cut him down to size. From what you say, his range must be between his home cabin and the country of the Crows. Narrows finding him considerable. Him and the boy. I'll show Lyman and toadyin' up to the Crows and them. Then I'll put him under and get the boy back. Wun't trouble me to have some help on the way. Particularly anybody Lyman's used the way you boys say he's used you. What do you say? Want to get in on it?"

"You mean us?" Butler asked, his turn to be incredulous.

"I don't mean Andy Jackson and the U.S. Congress."

"What about the word they got out on us?"

Skull's eyes narrowed on Butler. "Nobody's going to get you that you don't let get you! If I take anybody back up there with me, it'll be men! Not little boys that'll run snot-nose home to mama the first time somebody makes a fist at 'em. You'll listen and listen good and you'll learn and you'll fight. Else stay down here in this pig-slop."

"I'm for it," Will Dooley said bravely.

"Count me in," Butler concurred

Luke Farmer paused, thinking. "Me, too," he said.

Skull looked them over, sizing them up again. "All right. You'll take orders from me. No backtalk—we need plenty of money and fast to get outfitted and get moving. We start tonight and it may mean slitting a few throats. Is that clear?"

The three looked at each other and at him.

"Ah, yeah," Butler said, speaking for his partners.

"All right. Till then, we've got a couple of jugs to clear. Drink up! I think I about got enough left for another."

Chapter Fifteen

DANIEL STAYED WITH HIS NEW WIFE AND SHE AND HER SISTER, Grass Woman, and his mother and new mother-in-law readied their belongings for the journey to the 1836 rendezvous—on the Green River near Horse Creek. Meanwhile, Lyman and Walking Feather made a two-day inspection tour of the streams their council of friendly trappers and Indians had reserved for the beaver to raise their young.

"It is good for us to spend this quiet time together, Jacob," Walking Feather said beside their small but cheerful night fire on the second of three waterways dammed here and there along its length to form placid ponds with the beavers' humps of chewed-stick lodges in their middles. "But others watch us and wonder at our wisdom in setting aside such places for saving the beaver. There is anger and jealousy."

Jake studied the seamed, aging face of his Crow friend, the firelight reflecting the highlights and deepening the shadows in the seasoned, richly dark visage with its deep and thoughtful eyes.

In many ways, their unwieldy and often difficult cooperative experiment in conservation brought Jake great satisfaction and joy. Several times over the intervening year, he had been able, with a warming heart from the cover of streambank trees, to silently watch the beavers' and their kits' playful and often comical antics, content with the knowledge that their lives— for at least a year and because of him—were free of threat.

He'd never taken much time to study the beavers' habits with such leisure and enjoyment. Where before beaver were a business, a prey, now he had a stake in their growth and security, and the process delighted him.

It was good, so good, he thought, that lives—whether beaver, white man, or Indian—should be allowed the time and the freedom to develop with abundance and to have their moments of wild and happy splashing abandon and comedy. His plan—actually, he allowed, Marcus Whitman's—was a good one, a step, if only a small and tentative one, in the right direction.

Again and again over the year, he thought how much Whitman's inspired wisdom had brought clear and gratifying thinking into his life and with it beneficial and benevolent rewards. Attitudes growing out of his conversations with Whitman had hastened Daniel's emotional recovery to the point that Jake and Walking Feather—as well as Rachel and Moon-That-Grows—had given permission for the marriage of Daniel and Walking Feather's delightful oldest daughter, Soft Wind. It was solemnized in a Crow wedding dance, a festival of feasting and celebration of several days; when Marcus Whitman arrived at rendezvous, Jake planned to ask a minister certain to be in Whitman's party to sanctify their union in their eyes of the white man's God.

"Three small streams for you I and our friends who think as we do to watch over while the beaver multiply and grow is not so much to ask, and is only a start," Lyman told Walking Feather. "This start shall grow as men understand our purpose. Besides, there is nothing wrong with it. It is the code of first-come rights that the man with the first traps in the water, whether he is white or Indian, is respected. By decent men, anyway. Is it any different that we simply leave the animals untrapped a little longer? And we were here first!"

"I would understand that thinking," Walking Feather said. "Others do not. Some think Jacob and Walking Feather and our council of white trappers and Crows are fools. The beaver, like the buffalo, they say, are so numerous and multiply so fast that they will always be there for the harvest."

Lyman felt a spurt of indignation. They had a good and working plan—hard to control, perhaps—but he had muddleheaded friends among the white trappers as well who resisted or were doubtful, just as Walking Feather experienced with the Indians.

"But," Lyman insisted, "the beaver disappear into the traps faster than they can bear and raise their kits. White men come into this country now to shoot buffalo for a sport . . . like a game. They make wagers for who will kill the most in a day. We can do nothing about that. That is wrong—and harmful. But for the beaver, we must work that the seed is saved and the numbers multiply. This is why we must be strong and forceful, Walking Feather, without violence, to work for our goal. Those who do not understand this, Indian or white, must be persuaded by our good example to freely accept the worth and the promise of our venture."

Walking Feather regarded Jake silently for a long time. "Forever, until the coming of the white man, my people in the mountains and on the plains maintained a delicate balance with their surroundings."

Lyman came even more alert to Walking Feather's words; unbeknownst, his Indian friend used Whitman's very phrase!

Walking Feather was silent a long moment before he spoke. "The Circle of Life that begins with the round Sun and his brother, the lodge fire, and the lodgepole ring, extends to a place fouled and grazed that must be abandoned."

Lyman looked at him puzzled.

"The Circle of Life, Jacob," Walking Feather explained. "We foul the place where we live with our leavings. The horse crops the grass to the ground, but it strengthens the roots, and his droppings—like ours—replenish the land. We kill the buffalo to eat and the beaver for his plew. What we do not use melts back into the land to nourish grass and trees. We go away to a new place and the land we have wounded heals itself. The beaver and the buffalo come back stronger because there is room and food for new life."

Walking Feather stared another long moment into their night fire. "We—you and I—Jacob, are like the buffalo and the beaver and the grass and the trees. Soon we will be old, used up. We, too, are in the Circle of Life. It is in the plan that we, too, will return to the earth that gave us life and breath.

"My heart is good that Daniel has taken Soft Wind as his woman. Though he is not of Jacob Lyman's blood, he has taken the strength and the heart of Jacob as he has learned your ways. He is today as much your son as if he were grown from your seed. It is good now that our families are joined. In the strong sons and daughters of Soft Wind and Daniel, we will live on, you and I as one, brothers, Jacob." Walking Feather beamed at the prospect.

"Daniel's years among Indians help him understand and accept your ways. His feelings for Soft Wind are true. He will be a kind and considerate husband," Lyman said.

"Unlike some of my brothers, I do not feel that halfbreeds weaken blood lines. Blood—of whose blood we are—I think, does not make a man strong or weak. It is in how he comes to his manhood. Daniel had troubled years among his captors, but I have seen him turn it as a force for good in his life, with Jacob and Rachel as his strong guides. There are hotheads and troublemakers among young Indian men, too. And we have seen bad young white men in the three who attacked my daughters."

"Dr. Whitman will come to rendezvous with his new wife on their way to take his healing powers and his wisdom to the country of the Cayuse and the Nez Perce."

"He had better stay with Lyman's family and come to the country of the Crow people with his healing and his wisdom."

"We have already benefited from his healing and his wisdom," Jake said. "It was his thought that Jacob and Walking Feather should form a council to share our efforts and our learning and to make places for the beaver to grow, as we have here."

"We will talk with him at rendezvous," Walking Feather said, "and learn more from him before he leaves for the land of the Cayuse and the Nez Perce."

"Also last rendezvous," Jake added, "before he turned back to the east to marry and prepare for his life in our country, he gave me wisdom that has helped Daniel become a strong enough man to come to Walking Feather and ask for Soft Wind as his woman."

Walking Feather's eyes turned distant with thought, while a smile crinkled his mouth and his face.

"I find great delight with them in my heart," he said. "So grown, yet so much like children. Daniel watches me to learn how to become a good Indian husband. Soft Wind watches Rachel to learn how to become a good white wife! They will yet bring us much joy in our years, Jacob."

LYMAN RODE INTO the Horse Creek rendezvous a week later with his family and that of Walking Feather to find the giant, sprawling camp in a mood he had not known before, and in a frenzy of elaborate preparation. The word had been passed: Go easy on the Taos Lightnin' and get the finery ready for the big celebration.

Broken Hand Tom Fitzpatrick and his American Fur Company caravan were two days east along the Sweetwater, rendezvous-bound. With them were several wagons of the missionary party led by Dr. Marcus Whitman, become mountain-man legend as the hero of the Platte River cholera scourge and the skilled surgeon of the celebrated Bridger "arrahead" episode of last year's rendezvous—monumental events that gained new luster with each night-fire retelling.

To add to the jubilant anticipation, Whitman brought with him his new wife, Narcissa, another missionary couple, the Reverend Henry Spalding and Mrs. Eliza Spalding, and a fifth member of their party, a bachelor, William Gray, a carpenter and handyman with ambitions to become a minister and missionary.

It had been years for many of the mountain men since they'd seen a white woman, and these were women of the church and thus of high station and therefore destined to be accorded a respect and an awe that bordered on the extreme.

And the mountain men could be depended on to behave like clumsy, paddle-footed coonhound pups in demonstrating their esteem. To hear Joe Meek tell it, it had already begun.

Through the rendezvous camp of more than four hundred assembled mountain men and throngs of Indian men, women, and children from some fifteen Western tribes, Meek, buckskin-clad to the teeth, as self-appointed chairman of the welcoming committee, strutted around in high glee and importance as he made certain the sprawling grounds and the celebrants were in readiness for the red-letter day.

Meek was lately back from several days on the trail toward South Pass, impatient to verify that the Whitman party was indeed coming along with the fur company mule train.

Lyman found Meek holding forth at a well-attended talking fire in the middle of the camp.

"Wagh, boys," Meek began. "Just rode in this mawnin'. High old times! Some of you wa'n't here some days back afore we left. Bunch of us got the itch to ride on out along the Sweetwater to see what was holdin' up Broken Hand and the doctor and the church folks with the white ladies. Six or seven of us trappers there was, with ten, maybe twelve Nezz Pursees Indians, riding out the trail east.

"Spied the train afore they saw us, so we painted for a hellacious welcome, I'm here to tell you! I figured old Broken Hand and them'd take us for a war party was we to come up whoopin' and yellin' as we had calculated. I had old Doc Newell slide his rifle's wipin' stick out the thimbles just shy of losing it in the breeze and tied a white truce rag on the end and held up like a flagpole so the mountaineers in the train'd know we warn't a passel of hostiles there to raise hair.

"Down on them we rode, yellin' and screechin' up a storm. I suppose in their eyes and in their surprise our twelve and a half must've growed to a hundred charging down on them that way. Wagh! Reckon I'd've been scairt, too. And sure enough, they took us all for Indians!

"Old Broken Hand had them commence to fort up against attack and I worried that maybe them boys'd start taking a few potshots at us. We'd've been hoist by our own petard right then and there, and that's for certain! Along about then old Broken Hand spied Doc's white flag and set to grinnin'. Word passed along the train that it was just funnin' boys riding out from ronnyvoo. So then we let all hell break loose. We rode down the line of wagons firing our smokepoles at the sky, the fur men with the train yippin' and hootin' back at us in merry doin's."

Meek stifled a laugh, remembering.

"Old Doc Newell plumb forgot and touched off his Hawkins and his muzzle blast set that white rag on his ramrod a-scorchin' and a-smokin'! That there was a comical sight for these old eyes, I'm here to tell you!

"We wheeled around past the train and rode back again along the wagons making our horses to prance and rare up and sashay.

"It taken a while for those missionary people to settle down and get it through their heads that we weren't devildogs sent straight from hell. The ladies, maybe, were more quick to see the sport in it, particularly Miz Whitman. Miz Spalding got her smile back pretty quick, too. The men, particularly the Reverend Spalding and Mister Gray was a bit more edgewise towards us, and for longer. Doctor Whitman's been around us afore, so he took our foolishness in high glee. There's something eatin' on this Spalding toward the doctor and his wife that the sharp eye can see. It don't come out in the open, but it's there like bad blood.

"We rode with the train a couple of days, getting acquainted and paying our respects to those fine white ladies. Then we come on back here to get you boys primed for high doin's.

"We're asking, boys, that you walk soft with the Taos Lightnin' for a few days or do your drinking out of sight. And your reelin' and your stumblin'. They'll be gone in a little bit and we can get back to the larrupin' times.

"Be on your best behavior and respectful of their station with the white ladies in camp. Show them the respect you'd show your mother or your grandmother if either of them was to show up out here. Or your Sunday School teacher. Or your white wife, if ever you'd have one! Or one'd have you! Wagh!"

"What're they like, Joe?" a mountaineer by the campfire asked, his eyes unblinking and bright in curiosity. "The white ladies?"

"Oh, I tell you boys, these are shinin' times to remember. To tell your grandkids. Miz Whitman and Miz Spalding are grand ladies." Joe Meek's eyes went distant and misty with memory. "Miz Whitman, no mistaking her whenever the train arrives, is a tall and strong and grand lady and carries herself like the proper and proud Christian woman she is. Hair like a bay horse, light reddish-brown, what they call auburn. A pleasant, lively face. She's dignified, but not high-and-mighty; right off she makes a man feel relaxed and comfortable around her. Hear and heed her words, boys, for she speaks of Christian love and decency. You're all good, old coons, but there ain't a one of you boys couldn't learn something from her."

Meek paused to catch his breath and his memory.

"Miz Spalding is a leetle bird of a woman, pale-skinned and been feeling puny a lot of the time, I'm told. While Miz Whitman has been happy riding sidesaddle like the proper eastern lady she is most of the trip, Miz Spalding travels in their light wagon, called a Dearborn. But she's no weak woman! She don't shine to Miz Whitman for looks ner as right-off warm as Miz Whitman, but Miz Spalding has winning ways, I'm here to tell you. They are good people, all of them, with the proper intentions for the New West."

Chapter Sixteen

As Jake Lyman thought about it later, the reception couldn't have been grander if President Andy Jackson himself had been in that magnificent long-line procession of wagons and riders from the east lumbering into view of the Horse Creek rendezvous encampment. Joe Meek's ambitious welcome demonstration worked like a charm to create the most memorable event Lyman could remember of all the annual fur frolics.

Especially so, he thought, in light of the high degree of sobriety that marked this one; mountain-man faces were even shaved and scrubbed.

All around him, while his ears roared with the excited clamor, his eyes were dazzled by buckskins bright with colorful beads or quillwork and dangling, flapping whang-fringe, or by blousy and brilliant calico-print shirts of eye-catching reds, blues and yellows. Feet stepping out jauntily in fancy-beaded moccasins in distinctive Indian designs blended handsomely with waists encircled by wide, many-hued, finger-woven wool sashes. Here and there fancy-beaded hunting pouches rounded out a man's finery; powderhorns were brought to a high polish as well. Headgear was perched cocked and cocky, whether or fur or felt, and here and there the rakish and floppy wool-knit caps of the French-Canadian *voyageur* design appeared.

Burnished domed brass tacks glistened afresh on the stocks of St. Louis rifles or Northwest trade guns, their novel patterns bragged on by the owners, confident that the symbols made the guns shoot "plumb-center!"

To Jake Lyman's amused eyes, the rendezvous camp had pulled out all the stops.

The Indians, with even more traditional ways to festively adorn themselves, were not to be outdone by their white counterparts. Gleaming ebony hair of men, women, and children was groomed and braided, plaited fetchingly with strips of red flannel, and embellished with giant feathers of hawk, turkey, or eagle. Men and women draped themselves regally with showy red or green Hudson's Bay point blankets; hawk bells tinkled gaily on shirts and leggins. Chokers of short snow-white hare-pipes and multi-colored trade beads graced the dusky throat of many a brave, while others sported torso-covering breastplates of longer hare-pipes.

Ermine tails or pendent elks' teeth often festooned women's buckskin dresses.

Faces as well as favorite Indian ponies were painted in traditional designs and colors to symbolize celebration.

THE SUN WAS nearly at its zenith when a cry went up east of camp; the wagon train was in sight!

Horsemen, red and white, scrambled for their mounts while those afoot bent the grass that way at a lope ahead of the riders, with deafening roars of delight. Pandemonium took over in the mad dash to be among the first to "hoorraw" the newcomers.

Scores of Indians on horseback, most of them Meek's "Nezz Pursees," and a goodly number of mounted trappers at high gallop pounded past Lyman and his family with that of Walking Feather joining many others afoot to greet the wagon train at a more leisurely pace. The air around them was alive with the thunder of hooves, great shouts and cries, and the crisp barks of rifles pointed skyward in jubilation.

Daniel, hand-in-hand with Soft Wind and Grass Woman, stepped out ahead of their elders and quickly blended into the mob of trappers and Indians trudging out to greet the wagons. In the distance, well behind the long line of the fur company wagons, Lyman could see four of the missionaries on horseback. His spirit soared as even at a distance he recognized the bareheaded Marcus Whitman towering over and waving and calling enthusiastically to the cheering multitude clustered around his horse. Riding near him was the stately looking woman in black riding habit and mounted sidesaddle that must be, Lyman thought with glowing thrill, Mark's beloved Narcissa. Her uncovered auburn hair looked almost golden in the sun. His heart leaped as even at the distance he could see that Narcissa was everything Mark had described in a grand, dignified lady.

The mounted Indians and trappers rode the fringes of the crowd, unable to get close but then closing ranks behind the train to proudly follow en masse as it made its way toward the center of the rendezvous camp.

Striding along beside Jake, Walking Feather appeared as handsome as Lyman had ever seen him. He wore beaded moccasins and fringed leggins, also with strips of beadwork; his loins were modestly covered by a broad, deep-blue, wool breechclout with trailing ends that draped nearly to his knees. The tail of a brand-new red and yellow print calico shirt was tucked in his waistband. A necklace that was a many-tiered cascade of strands of short hare pipes threaded on sinew dangled across and down his chest. In anticipation of the grand event, Walking Feather lately had traded beaver plews for a new broad and stiff-brimmed brown felt hat with a low, rounded crown, and that he now fitted straight to his head. His long, obsidian hair hung in two braids over his ears, tied off at the ends with red flannel.

Lyman's heart soared. Walking Feather, strong as ever in his convictions and his style as a Crow Indian, was trying in his dress to indicate his willingness and his openness to receive the white man's teachings and ways and to learn and grow in the process. His and Whitman's crude plan, he thought, might be working at last.

Chattering away in Crow dialect with the animation of eastern housewives, Rachel and Moon-That-Grows followed a few paces behind their husbands.

Within moments, the once-again startled missionaries— three men and two women—their wagons and spooky herd of domestic cattle were surrounded by cheering, enthusiastic throngs. Jake, along with Walking Feather, Rachel, and Moon-That-Grows held back, content to watch the activity from a distant hillside.

"I hope I may speak with Jacob's friend, Dr. Whitman," Walking Feather said as they watched the mounting activity before them. "I will ask him to keep his cattle and his wagons in the land of the Crow so that he may teach us the white man's way and the way of the white man's God."

"He must go to Oregon, Walking Feather," Lyman explained as patiently as he could, "where his friend of last rendezvous, Reverend Parker, has already gone ahead to start his teachings among the Cayuse and the Nez Perce."

"Then I will ask Doctor Whitman to send more shamans and head men of the white man's God and his medicine men to come and live among the Crows to cure us of the white man's poxes and to remove arrowheads and bullets, and so that we may learn from their teachings."

Lyman hoped he could explain clearly. "Higher authority than Doctor Whitman has decreed that their teachings should be with the Oregon tribes of the Nez Perce and the Cayuse and not stop halfway. The mission people do not possess great riches to do their teaching everywhere."

Lyman was not prepared for the edge in Walking Feather's normally docile voice. "Below me, my eyes tell me differently, Jacob. These missionaries have abundance in cattle herds and need three wagons for their belongings. Do the Nez Perce and the Cayuse need to learn how to gain white man's riches and white man's privileges more than do the Crow, who even since the times of their fathers have tried to live in peace with the white man in this country and the evil traders? We have been here, among the beaver—the white man's riches—his trading forts and his waterways since his first coming, and suffered his whiskey, his trickery, and his poxes. Why should the Crow after all this not be first to learn to gain from the white man's teachings and the saving words of his God?"

Lyman's heart sank. "Do you think that's what it's about, Walking Feather? Riches and privileges? Is that all there is? Do you think that's what our council is about and our letting the beaver grow and prosper so our later trapping can be more abundant, only to gain more riches?"

"This is what my eyes tell me of the white man's ways."

Lymans mind spun in turmoil. Just when he thought he had the Indian mentality figured out, he found himself confronted with such examples of simple logic. It had nothing to do with intelligence; the man beside him had a common-sense brand of wisdom that bordered on brilliance. What it did have to do with was a directness that did not fully comprehend deceit.

As he thought of it, this was the very ingredient in the muddled matrix of white-Indian relationships that allowed the unscrupulous traders and trappers to lure the native tribesman into dependency on snakehead whiskey and to bilk him out of his hard-earned beaver pelts for handfuls of trinkets. Outright evil the Indians could understand; oily lies they seemed to fall for lock, stock, and barrel.

How could he explain to this direct-thinking man—his friend—that the means—the gathering of wealth—justified the end—a happier, more abundant life? In Walking Feather's eyes, the white man's life of "riches and privileges," compared to his, the means were an end in themselves; listen to the white man's talk and teachings of God and industry and surely the thing the Indian most envied—the riches—would follow. This seemed to Lyman to be what Walking Feather's logic told him.

He remembered Mark Whitman's shrewd observation that right-thinking, understanding whites were superior in that they were "masters of the means" of helping Indians to assimilate and adjust to the coming white tide without totally sacrificing their culture or their dignity. He also suddenly wondered if gentle, well-intentioned men like Marcus Whitman were not like the voice of one crying in the wilderness, as in the Book of Matthew, to prepare the way of the Lord and make his paths straight.

Or, Lyman wondered, would anyone out here in this wilderness of the West ever hear and heed the voice of righteousness?

Suddenly he had a desperate need to speak alone and in depth with Marcus Whitman. Mark could be relied upon to listen, understand and wisely counsel Jake in dealing with his friend, Walking Feather.

For the moment, he set aside his troubling talk with Walking Feather and threw an arm around Rachel's shoulders. "Let's get down there, Missus Lyman!" he said loudly and cheerfully. "Doctor and Missus Whitman must wonder why we are not among their early greeters!"

Together the four walked down the low hill and blended into the crowd of well-wishers parting on either side to make way for the wagon train.

The Whitmans were off their horses, leading them as they walked beside their creaking, mule-drawn wagons, responding to the greetings of the still-noisy crowds along the way.

The Spaldings had moved away from the Whitmans to greet trappers and Indians alike, though there was less of a crowd around them than thronged the Whitmans.

Rev. Spalding was some taller than his pale, thin but bright-eyed and alert wife. Both of them were dark-haired, Rev. Spalding the more imposing-looking of the two. For his days on the trail, he wore the gray shirt and trousers of a farmer with sturdy boots designed for walking much of the way west. He was a fierce-eyed man with a high forehead and shoulder-length hair worn full around the ears and neck. His strong, slanting eyebrows and full black beard lent a further diabolical cast to his expression. Almost in contrast, Eliza, with bird-like frailty but with a nervous kind of energy greeted all with intense warmth and compassion written in her eyes and in her expression.

Narcissa had found herself surrounded by awed and admiring Indian women, curious but courteous, who'd never seen a woman of such fair complexion or hair coloring before. A beaming Joe Meek escorted and protected her while her husband, a short distance away, was preoccupied with greetings and introductions and chatting as he beamed unending smiles and engaged in robust conversations with acquaintances and strangers alike.

The missionaries' wagons now were stopped at the edge of camp while the fur company's train under Fitzpatrick's guidance rumbled on to a convenient place to set up the trading tables, their lodges, the fur presses, and to get down to business.

Whitman, still leading his horse, caught sight of Jake and Rachel in the clamoring crowd, his eyes lighting up in delight as he broke away politely from his admirers of the moment and made his way toward them.

Beside them, Walking Feather spoke up. "I will take Moon to speak with Mrs. Whitman," he said, an excitement and anticipation in his voice. "Daniel has helped me with English words of greeting and the proper way to speak with such a woman. Jacob, we will speak later with Doctor Whitman."

"Do say hello to Mrs. Whitman," Lyman said heartily. "Rachel and I will join you soon."

While Walking Feather and Moon-That-Grows disappeared into the crowd, Lyman grabbed Rachel's hand to lead her to meet Mark Whitman, forcing his way toward them.

"Jake!" Whitman called as they drew near enough to speak, "You don't know how I've longed for this moment!" He came near enough to reach for Lyman's hand to shake, and to reinforce his sincerity by clutching Jake's forearm with his left.

"And our dear Rachel! God, how I've missed you! The Divine Angel of Bellevue!"

Around them, understanding the needs of the moment, trappers and Indians formed a tight but open circle around the three of them for this moment of grand reunion; all knew of the roles the Lymans had played in the miraculous work of the legendary doctor from the East.

Whitman turned, beaming, to Rachel to grasp her forearms affectionately, looking deeply into her eyes. "Oh, the Savior surely dwells within thee!" Impulsively, he pulled her toward him for a magnificent hug; Rachel blushed, but responded with her arms gripping Whitman.

"Doctor Whitman, you've been missed out here, too!" she said, her eyes overflowing with love and delight, and fixed on Jake's over Whitman's shoulder.

Almost as impulsively, Whitman released Rachel. "Jake and Rachel! You must excuse me. My 'adoring public,' you know. Make yourselves known to my Narcissa. She could scarcely wait to meet you."

He looked at both of them. "Jake! When all this calms down, we must talk. Perhaps tonight at whatever lodgings I have. I think Fitzpatrick is raising a tent for us."

"And I need to speak with you, Mark." Lyman responded.

"I hope it's good tidings. Mine aren't." With that, Whitman turned away from them and returned to his contacts with the admiring crowd.

Rachel gripped Jake's hand as the crowd again swirled around them and Marcus Whitman disappeared into its midst.

"What was that all about, Jake?" she asked.

"Search me," was the response. "But I'll know more before long."

* * *

NOT FAR FROM them across the noisy congestion of crowded men, Walking Feather, with Moon-That-Grows smiling in her self-consciousness at his side, caught Narcissa's attention; her comforting smile back at them relieved their nervousness. As Daniel had advised, Walking Feather ducked his head as he politely doffed his large hat by the brim and held it in front of himself.

"Mrs. Whitman," he began in his halting English, as coached by Daniel England. "I am Walking Feather of the Crows, the friend of Jacob Lyman. May I present my woman, Moon-That-Grows." This was all he had been prepared for, and understood but a word here and there of her response.

"Walking Feather!" she proclaimed loudly but with a supreme grace, reaching out to take both of their hands in hers and holding them as she studied them with great interest. She was slightly taller than both of them, but stood with an amiable dignity and warmth they both could feel. "And Moon-That-Grows!" They both now understood their names spoken in English and were astonished to hear the words. "I've heard so much about you and of Soft Wind and Grass Woman. I trust we will see much of each other these next few days. And talk. I pray your daughters are strong after the attack upon them last year."

Walking Feather understood the gist of her words and explained them to Moon. He wished he had had Daniel give him more words to tell the grand Mrs. Whitman of their pride in the marriage of Rachel and Jacob's son with their daughter, Soft Wind. But, he reasoned, that would come in time and he could watch her eyes for the hoped-for delight he expected in them.

They had taken enough of Mrs. Whitman's time to suit some of the other Indian women and they began clamoring for her attention. "I hope to meet Jacob and Rachel before long," she called, turning her attention away from them to the admiring but demanding Indian women. Walking Feather looked happily and gratified at Moon and led her away into the crowd.

THE SEETHING AND the shouting had died down by the time Marcus Whitman sought out Jake Lyman at Walking Feather's lodge. As he entered the tapering circle of pale yellow firelight dancing against the lodgeskins, he acknowledged Walking Feather seated at the back or west arc of the lodge's perimeter, and Rachel, Moon-That-Grows and Soft Wind and Grass Woman on his right. He moved directly to join Jake and Daniel on stacks of buffalo robes on the south side.

"Before we get on with anything, Jake," he said, taking a seat beside Lyman, "it's urgent that I tell you what I know. Perhaps you can explain to Walking Feather in his tongue in a moment."

Lyman watched him with deep interest.

"At Fort Laramie one night, some of the *engagees* had been out drinking and came back to warn me."

"What this about, Mark?" Lyman started impatiently.

"I get ahead of myself. It was all the talk in New York State while Narcissa and I completed our preparations this past spring. This man Skull you told me of last year . . ."

Lyman looked at Daniel who now took considerable interest in Dr. Whitman's words.

"He killed two guards, one brutally, extremely brutally, shot the other in cold blood, and escaped the state penitentiary. Farther west in the state some days later, near the Pennsylvania line, it was apparent that he struck again, viciously killing a simple farmer, abusing his wife by securely chaining her in a cold barn. Then he viciously ravaged their adolescent daughter. They knew it was this Skull for he left his prison clothing and took that of the dead farmer."

Lyman heard Rachel gasp.

"Fitzpatrick's men came to tell me they saw Skull late at night outside Fort Laramie in a drinking place with three young men.

"If he's out here, he's up to no good," Jake said.

"It's even worse. The three men with him sound a great deal like those three that attacked Daniel and Walking Feather's daughters a year ago!"

Chapter Seventeen

SOFT WIND'S VOICE WAS AS GENTLE AND PRETTY AS HER name, her face, and her form. Narcissa Whitman found her an attractive young woman with a characteristic strength molded into her Indian features, which at the same time were delicate and feminine; her dark eyes reflected equal levels of gentility and drive in their unfathomable depths. Soft Wind had come with Rachel to visit Narcissa. In the missionary couple's large home-made conical tent of oiled bed ticking, she came to listen and to try out her rudimentary English. Even before their marriage ceremony, Daniel had worked with her on learning the language of the white people. In turn, Soft Wind helped Daniel develop his proficiency in the Crow dialect. They pondered—in their hopeful, ambitious, and intimate newlywed hours—that together they might make a difference, lending their support to Lyman's and Walking Feather's attempts at breaking down barriers between white men and Indians.

"I try, yes, to be good with my English," Soft Wind said, her words clear as the crystal tinkle of her voice, her eyes probing deeply into Narcissa's. "It needs great practice," she added sweetly, almost breathless with the effort, but smiling softly and confidently.

Mrs. Whitman, whose proud bearing was not intimidating, reached out lovingly to rest her palm on Soft Wind's hand. Her eyes reaching into the young woman's glowed with care and concern. "You do very well, my dear," she said. "Try when you can to understand the work of the Lord, Jesus. I wish I had the time to stay and help you to read that you might understand and benefit from the nourishment of the Scriptures."

Near them as they sat on folding wood and canvas chairs such as she had seen in Rev. Parker's tent the year before, Rachel basked in the glow of visiting with the first white woman she had seen in more than seven years. Her nervous anticipation was quickly put at ease by Narcissa's gracious welcome and engaging manner. At once, the rough nature of the surrounding wilderness and the rendezvous camp seemed to be miles away. The nostalgic remembrance of that other life of home, family and friends—now as remote in time as it was in distance and in kind—swirled back in a rush of memory.

The momentary hope—or prayer—crossed her mind that the venture of this fine woman into the hostile West would not result in such tragedy as she had endured. A sudden chill ran through her with the occurrence of such a dark notion.

"Jacob has a Bible among several books at our home in the mountains," she said, her thoughts coming back to the here and now. "When Soft Wind comes with Daniel, or the next time Jacob and I come to be with them or with Walking Feather's family, I'll bring it and work with her in reading and read to her."

Narcissa smiled. "I think I can remedy the situation even sooner. We have with us a number of new Bibles. I will ask Husband to fetch one from the wagons for Soft Wind's very own. I'm afraid they are not handsomely bound, though."

Rachel smiled back. "Proof of the old adage of not judging a book by its cover."

Narcissa chuckled. "Verily." She paused for a long moment, studying Rachel. "Husband has told me at great length, Rachel, of your sufferings and those of Daniel until Jake came into your lives and managed to reunite you. What a happy ending to a wonderful story of courage and love . . . which is not to gloss over the extreme suffering mother and son must have endured."

"Jacob was the brilliant and beautiful rainbow at the end of a long and terrifying storm."

"God's sometimes extreme ways of testing our strength and our faith are often hard to comprehend. Your courageous faith was its own reward."

"I shall always miss Edwin, my first husband. My decision to marry Jacob, however, was not out of any sense of obligation. My love for him I can assure you, is as true as it is deep and abiding."

"God also tests me, Rachel," Narcissa confessed. "Oh, leaving the bosom of home and family left me with great misgivings. But the adventure! The challenge of bringing the news of God's love and salvation into these remote lands! The goal made the uprooting and the rude life of camp and trail more lustrous than laborious! A grand passion!"

"How then does God test you, Narcissa?"

The grand lady smiled benignly. "Not nearly to the length or extent of your travail to be sure, Rachel. But my forbearance has been tested almost daily. Not with Husband nor Mr. Gray nor Liza Spalding, in whom I share great kinship in our work and in God's love."

"You seem to purposely exclude the Reverend Spalding." Rachel did not mean to sound accusing, but only to acknowledge her inkling of Narcissa's quandary.

"Nothing particularly dark or sinister. I hide nothing from Husband, nor from Liza Spalding. Henry Spalding was smitten with me, I'm afraid more deeply than I realized, years ago when we were theology students back home. Henry comes from a very troubled childhood and youth. In our conversations as young and eager students, I tried to strengthen his conversion to Christ and his convictions to work in the service of the Lord.

"Henry seems to feel the relationship developed more deeply and that there was some sort of understanding between us which, so help me, I never meant to encourage. He has

since been openly embittered over my 'spurning' and makes
vicious, hateful remarks far and wide about me and about my
family, especially my father who he is certain persuaded me to
discourage his advances. His spite is so senseless and cuts so
very, very deep.

"To forgive is divine, but of anyone on this earth, dear
Rachel, whom I would not have sought to make this ardu-
ous trip with, and to help Husband and me build a future in
Christ in the Oregon country, it would have been Henry
Harmon Spalding!"

"I understand now why you feel that God tests you."

"In God's love, all things are possible," Narcissa replied,
brightening with the thought. "It's relief in itself, Rachel,
after all these trying months, to unburden myself with you.
Husband has been understanding. For obvious reasons, I
skirt the issue in my dealings with Liza Spalding, though
not to be devious. Only sensitive. Talking it out with her
would accomplish little. You indeed are the angel Husband
so glowingly described to me last winter when he returned
home. He so wished that you and Jake and Daniel could
have witnessed our wedding in February. Would you like to
hear the hymn sung by the congregation after we repeated
our vows? The words were uncommonly appropriate."

"Oh, yes!"

"It was "Yes, My Native Land, I Love Thee.""

Narcissa looked off at the side of the tent remembering.
She sang the verses softly but with great beauty:

Yes, my native land! I love thee;
All thy scenes I love thee well;
Friends, connections, happy country,
Can I bid you all farewell?
Can I leave you,
Far in heathen lands to dwell?

"In the deserts let me labor,
On the mountains let me tell,
How He died—the blessed Savior—
To redeem the world from hell!
Let me hasten,
Far in heathen lands to dwell!"

Only Soft Wind's eyes were dry as Narcissa finished her hymn, and then only because of her scant understanding of English.

"And now . . . soon . . . we go on to get to the work before us." Narcissa reached out and caught hold of Rachel's hand, looking deeply into her eyes.

"You are such a dear friend, Rachel. I've felt I knew you well for so many months and now as we sit face to face and chat, my feelings are confirmed. Because of that, may I be permitted another confession? A very special secret? I've not yet confided in Husband!"

Rachel's heart leaped; she knew the secret from the thrust of Narcissa's words, but gave her the opening to reveal it. She put her other hand reassuringly over Narcissa's holding hers. "Of course."

"In this year of 1836, I am twenty-eight years old and though I have spurned a great many suitors—even, I suppose, Henry Spalding—I thought for some years I might, in my choosiness, become an old maid. Then Marcus Whitman entered my life and in great excitement and love, I've been able to put all that behind me. It has been difficult in these months of laborious travel to be together as husband and wife. Always someone near and always after a day of travel, totally exhausted after making camp and meals and tending to stock, wanting nothing more of the bed than to sleep."

A sly smile crept into Narcissa's face.

"But here and there we found opportunities. And I am not too old! God blesses our union!"

Rachel reached out from her chair to grasp Narcissa's shoulders in an emotional hug of joy. Again, their eyes were moist while Soft Wind, again not comprehending, watched them dry-eyed and with a puzzled look.

Rachel, recognizing her daughter-in-law's confusion, spoke to her in Crow. "Mrs. Whitman will have a child."

Soft Wind smiled knowingly. She spoke in her halting English. "Then we are sisters. I have had the signs. I will have a child, too!"

Chapter Eighteen

"THIS IS JUST FOR OLD TIMES' SAKE, MARK," LYMAN SAID happily, tossing a stone to thunk into the stream. "Or have you been so busy you don't remember?"

"A man that's been to see the elephant don't easy forget, hoss," Whitman said, affecting a mountain-man twang. "The two of us. A year ago. We had a fine chat that day. Only then it was by New Fork, on the eve of my return east. Now we're on Horse Creek, and shortly I'll be on the last leg of my trip northwest to Oregon!"

"A lot's happened. You're married, Daniel's married and both your wives are in a family way. Walking Feather's and our council is working—with no particularly great strides, except that we have three streams nearby to Walking Feather's village in Crow country spending a year untrapped. The beaver are having lots of little ones, too."

"As I told you last year, Jake, sometimes these things take twice as long as you plan and are half as satisfying. Even after a year, if you have the three streams set apart and honored, you've made substantial progress. Think on that."

"Oh, don't get me wrong, Mark. I'm pleased about it and what's more, Walking Feather's Indians are mostly persuaded of the goodness of the idea. And partial to more time in council sessions and learning. Daniel and Soft Wind are excited about instructing the Crow in English. We've had talks with Walking Feather's people about watching out for unscrupulous traders."

"You'll make enemies, Jake. Be wary. There'll be Indians who won't understand your intrusion. The traders particularly will resent you for cutting into their ill-gotten gains."

"I've already got enemies in this country. Remember Skull's on the loose. And those three misbegotten misfits that ride with him. Not a one of them but wouldn't have a victory dance if my hair hung from a coup stick. Some of the company men and free trappers grumble, but they'd complain anyway about anything that didn't put more plews in their packs with the least amount of work. But thanks for the warning just the same."

"You've lived out here long enough to know the signs and you've led men to triumph over evil."

"I mind my backtrail and my flanks, Mark. But I can't be anything but excited about what's ahead!"

"Like Narcissa's and my grand quest in Oregon, you're onto something important and good. It'll grow. Slowly at first. Agonizingly so. Think of your progress so far! Then remember this conversation a year from now!"

"I'm sure I'll see the results. I've already seen them. I've traveled the streams twice this year, Mark. Just a few weeks ago with Walking Feather. We had such shinin' times together, seeing the progress and growth along the rivers, and making comforting night camps with good food and good talk beside a warm fire. Something about it that nourishes and inspires a man. Good and upright and decent. Greed put aside. All told, a fine experience. Watching the beaver teaching their young. And frolicking happy just for the hell of it. Just feeling free of fear! I've witnessed it from hiding when it was quiet as an empty church. So quiet, sometimes, Mark, it was hard to get my breath. Do you know such moments? Of joy and of peace? So beautiful. Their behavior and their water play. So contented and carefree. They're magnificent little creatures, comical and bucktoothed waifs that they are! And you know they're safe. They seem to know it too. Because of me, mostly. Well, us; you and me. It was your idea. But it surely puts a man in a new and bright mood. Of cleanliness. A clean and warm soul. A soul satisfied to be at rest and peace. And hopeful about things."

"Then can you imagine the satisfaction of a Christian missionary bringing in the sheaves?"

"Another comparison that's hard for an old hivernant like me to understand, Mark."

"But we're on the right track, Jake! Remember you are *master of the means* to bring the richness of life to these Indians and to prepare them for the challenge and ordeal of white invasion of their lives and lands that builds in the east like a giant explosion! I've seen it and I shrink in the face of its power! Yet all I can do is decent work and guidance in the name of Christ, and it is still a simple and weak voice in the wilderness most often misunderstood and shouted down. And when that voice is mismanaged, as it often is, it builds animosity; sometimes savage animosity.

"When that mounting explosion building in the East bursts, Jake, this land will be overrun like the Scriptural Great Flood. Right now, it only awaits more taming of the West, a little more widening of the old trails and the breaking of new ones. Don't you think for a moment that I haven't contemplated the potential hazards of our being here. The wave of the future we represent could be calamitous if not properly managed."

Whitman turned quiet with the depth of his thoughts. He looked out upon the placid river and like Lyman felt the almost reverent hush that lay on the land. Lyman saw the tightness of Whitman's features reflecting a great turmoil inside him.

"In the name of God, Jake, these humble creatures must be girded up! It's hard for me to fathom even in my own soul the extent of the trials they'll face. Even now we are probably too late in preparing them! In facing my own torment about it, I feel like a vulnerable David with a dismal bag of stones and a crude sling confronting a mighty Philistine

Goliath with his shield and sword. And I do not know that I have David's unerring aim nor Job's patience."

"If there were only more like you, Mark."

"We do what we can, Jake. With our frail wisdom and meager strength, and seeking God's blessing. On another subject, what about you, Jake? You and Rachel?"

"Have a child, you mean?"

"You read my mind."

"Ah, I don't know, Mark. I'm thirty-five. As we say, a bit long in the tooth for child-rearing. We've not really discussed it. We've been so involved with Daniel's return and our concern over his actions—his adjustment—after such an ordeal. But it worked. We'd not have considered consenting to his marriage if we hadn't felt he'd made remarkable progress. Besides, Rachel's thirty-four with an eighteen-year-old son, soon nineteen. She's going to be a grandma before long."

Whitman doubled up one knee as he sat on the streambank and held it with both hands, smiling now, and relaxed. "Your situation differs only in slight degree from mine, old friend. I'll be thirty-four in a month. Narcissa will be twenty-nine when our baby arrives."

"Rachel has five years on Narcissa. She's exceedingly strong and healthy, in spite of her ordeal as a captive. So far, nothing's happened with Rachel," Jake said. "I suppose it could. But, if she got in a family way even in the foreseeable future, the uncle or aunt would be still younger than the niece or nephew. Doesn't quite seem normal."

"Tell me anything that is anymore, Jake. Or optimistic."

"You lead me back to another subject. If our conservation efforts take hold, the beaver could make a comeback."

"It has to. Tom Fitzpatrick told me while we traveled together that ten years ago—in 1826—the Hudson's Bay people harvested 2,000 beaver. Last year, 1835, they reported only a mere 220. I don't see how their ship can stay afloat."

Lyman glowed with pride. "I estimate we've a good deal more than 200 that will mature for the spring hunt when we open the streams to trapping again. We've already decided on four streams we'll reserve next year. I hate to see those little fellers die, but I'm content when I think that even more of their brothers will enjoy a happy, abundant year in other areas. The beaver market is still sinking, but as you predicted, we'll compensate for that with richer harvests for the free white trappers and the Crows in our alliance!"

"I must get back, Jake. So much to do in three days before our departure. I spoke with Reverend Spalding about the wedding, by the way."

Lyman was self-absorbed watching a small, dark speck of hawk in an azure sky, wings stretched against cottony clouds, circling, now and again expertly waggling its wings as it sought the updraft to take it to even greater heights in lazy spirals on locked, extended wings. Like Lyman's protected beaver, the hawk reveled in the thing it enjoyed most—unbridled freedom. Lyman's eyes turned back to Whitman's.

"I hope it didn't put you in an awkward spot, Mark. It's much like the disapproval Rachel and I faced with Reverend Parker last year at Bellevue. Maybe even more ticklish with what you've told me of his stubborn attitude toward you and Narcissa."

"Spiteful would be closer to the truth. Though he's stubborn as well. I persuaded him that with no appropriate clergy available, they were wed with the blessing of all four parents and in a ceremony acceptable to the Crow tribe. I may have fibbed a little in describing that as the recognized civil authority in these lands. Thus the union is neither unlawful nor immoral. Somehow I persuaded him of my logic."

Jake grinned. "You have the makings of a sly old fox, Dr. Whitman!"

"I further assured him that the parents were strongly desirous, emphasizing the wishes of the Indian mother and father, that the vows be spoken and witnessed in the sight of the white man's God. Because he's anxious to bring the word of God to the 'heathen,' this will be his first such official act, and that aspect swayed him. We've set the day after tomorrow."

"Rachel will be delighted! She and Narcissa and Moon-That-Grows have talked of nothing else. Let's do it at your tent . . . before a small company. No need to make it another big hoopla. Mrs. Spalding's presence would be appreciated. Would Reverend Spalding think it a stronger Christian ceremony if Mr. Gray were there as well?"

"Certainly couldn't hurt. Let's get back and start the arrangements."

WHILE THE LYMAN, Whitman and Walking Feather families glowed with pride as Daniel and Soft Wind England repeated their marriage vows before a dour-faced Rev. Henry H. Spalding, a half-breed Crow and French-Canadian boy named Andre, living with his mother in Walking Feather's village many miles north of the rendezvous encampment, went running.

Andre, who could not remember his father, grew up living to run. He was a fine runner, the best in his village. It was the one thing he was better at than any of the boys, especially those he despised for their vicious tongues.

Younger by a year than Walking Feather's daughter, Grass Woman, who was fifteen, Andre was a quiet but gentle boy who mostly kept to himself. He had friends among Crow boys his age but was excluded by others who were rude to him because of his mixed blood.

Running was not running away, but had become a proper response when he was humiliated by those vicious tongues. He had tried physical response to verbal abuse and wound up with his body as well as his spirit bruised.

Andre had no reason for shame because of what he was nor who he was. He had been told that his father was a good man who had loved him and lived with Andre's mother's family among the Crows. He had also been told that his father had failed to return from a month-long trapping trip when Andre was only an infant. His father was not heard from again.

When the hurt of rejection and ridicule brought the old familiar bitter-squeezing in his belly and the anger-tightness in his chest, Andre disappeared running and free into the woods and fields and along the stream-sides, trails well-known because he'd run among them so often in his humiliation.

Running fleet and lonely as the wind cleansed his spirit and made him strong to rise above the cruel rejection of what he was, not who he was. He did not run only when he was sad. Running anytime brought Andre feelings of excellence and competence and challenge and helped him enjoy who he was; a whole and free person.

In some places, he'd made his own running trails to take advantage of fallen trees he could leap over as loose and free as the prairie antelope. As much as running itself, Andre loved the feeling of vaulting over the fallen trees—a sensory thrill that seemed to promise that, if he could only leap higher, he might catch an updraft and soar freely like the hawks and the eagles.

A great distance from the cluster of tall, cone-shaped lodges he called home, a favored trail followed a stream he had been warned to avoid. The village elders and white men, he was told, protected it to encourage the beaver to grow and multiply. Andre had trouble understanding this since the village elders and the white trappers made much of killing the beaver and taking the cured skins somewhere to trade for useful things.

Today, bitter and resentful and rebellious, Andre had run a great distance with malice festering as a great sore inside him. After a taxing run, he found himself alongside the closest of these streams. At an easy, loose-gaited trot, he followed a meandering trail that traced the bank and the beaver ponds—a pathway broken by trappers before and now by the elders who watched that no harm came to the beaver.

The industrious animals built many dams along the river trail Andre knew in his running. Many times, when he was there to run, he had stopped quietly and watched them at work. They were free to go about their work and play without cruel hurting words and actions of rejection, and he felt a kinship with the beavers.

He sensed something amiss at the first pond he neared as he trotted, his body drenched in sweat, his spirit cleansed now of the sourness and the outrage that had consumed him when he had left the village.

The sight before him was so shocking and obscene that his breath was stopped in his throat.

The sturdy dam was now badly broken—open down to the old stream bed. Water poured through this breach, rendering the pond a barren mudflat, the domed beaver lodge exposed high and dry. In the drying slime two full-grown beaver lay dead with slick, brown, and muddy fur garishly painted with blood, their tiny innocent eyes open and staring. Three smaller beavers lay nearby, lifeless in the thick brown ooze.

The crackle of gunfire from far upstream brought Andre's senses to keen alert. Other beavers must be being killed. This was not the method or the season for Crow or white trappers to kill beaver.

A strange surge of responsibility welled within him. He loved the beaver and that love—as his spirit had been many times—had been violated.

His mind was in turmoil with but another burning thought—the decisions of the village elders and the white trappers about saving the beaver were also violated. He was Crow and he was white; in some eyes, he was less than either. Still, everything good he stood for was somehow in jeopardy.

He had to know to go back and spread the alarm. He would be honored for that and perhaps the cruel voices would stop. He resumed his jog-trot upstream of the chaos of the first beaver home. As he ran, fear keeping a grip on his senses, his winding path took him past two more beaver dams, their lodges and occupants similarly ravaged. His heart sank. What evil was responsible for this vile chaos?

At the fourth, he emerged into a clear view of two white men in dirt-gray buckskins tearing furiously at another beaver dam.

At the edge of the water, two men waited, with rifles at the ready, to kill terrorized beaver emerging to escape. One of the buckskinned men on the bank wore a full crudely dried coyote pelt for a hat—the flattened nose and empty slanted eye-slits over his forehead, the pelt and tail trailing down his back. The other was hatless and older, his head strangely and startlingly barren of any kind of hair.

Andre pulled to a stop in full view of the four men, his good sense and terror telling him to turn and run back.

"Hey!" a voice yelled in the unknown white man's words. "It's an Injun. Git 'im!"

Andre, turning to flee back down the trail, felt a force—like a viciously swung lodgepole—slam his back. His ears defined the crisp crack of a rifle; instantly his lungs were bright with an intolerable seizure of pain. The sharp sear of strangling congestion gripped his chest and throat. The impact sent him reeling headlong into the rude grit of the trail. Terror drove him to his feet. Another rifle-roar slammed paralysis into his hips, and he fell again, feeling great humiliation at the outrage. A strong voice from within screamed at him to get up and run.

He staggered to his feet, wobbling, staggering, shuffling, ignoring agony, swinging legs that would not obey, groping in the blindness of pain for supporting tree trunks.

"Don't let the son-a-bitch git away!"

Another gun erupted with the distant, ill-defined pulsating shock of roar again, its blast far away in the misty awareness—like the sounds that first alerted him at the desecrated beaver pond. The sound burst over him with a serious, stunning thud to the head but was strangely without pain.

He'd bumped a tree limb, maybe. The periphery of his eyes caught sight of scattering bits of reddish bone attached to strands of long black hair flying ahead of him and around him. How could it be? Death? As he fell again he was also lifted up, light as though only his spirit lived.

A soaring sense of power came over him. His locked hips freed and he ran fleet as he had never run before; a giant log blocked his path and he soared over it and flew higher. And higher. At once he was over the trees, safe from the paralyzing rifle shots and free of the force that bound him and made him a slave to earth. Forever free of harsh, unkind words. The wind whistled around him, a clean, scouring source, purging his spirit of anger and resentment for all time; he felt whole and new and powerful.

His shoulder blades flexed and his extended arms sprouted wings that caught updrafts to elevate him to dizzying heights. He soared with the hawks, up, up, and up. Marks on the land grew smaller and land's horizon swelled to an infinity-arc meeting blue sky until he reached the clouds, soft and fluffy at first, then swiftly dense and dark. He felt the wind-spirit that held him there so buoyantly suddenly release its support like a rejecting evil demon. He fell, a long and slanted agonizing and plummeting descent and he tensed and his eyes closed on darkness in suffocating terror against the sudden drop.

Betrayed again!

Chapter Nineteen

TWO DAYS AFTER THE WHITMAN PARTY DEPARTED WITH guides to seek out the Oregon Trail and their destination, Jake answered an urgent summons to Walking Feather's lodge. A Crow rider from Walking Feather's village far to the north had come in great haste with distressing news.

With the first words, Lyman gasped in shock as he felt fury stiffen his body; his gnashing teeth resounded in his head.

His bold plan had been thwarted—viciously.

The rider who'd brought the news stayed to report the details in full.

"The beaver dams are no more, Jacob," Walking Feather intoned, his own ordeal of grief printed in tight, constricted features. "All of them. Torn down. Some lodges burned to drive out the beaver. Big mess. Bad. All three rivers. The beaver shot and wasted. My heart is heavy. For more than beaver.

"Eagle Tail, this man," Walking Feather explained, pointing to the Crow rider, "tells me that a young man of the village, a fine young man, a fierce runner, a mixed-blood, must have found the evil ones at the destroying and the killing and was shot three times before he died. Part of his head was blown away."

It was custom in many tribes to avoid mention of the deceased's name ever again.

Lyman was beside himself. His head drooped and he stared between his crossed legs at the hard-packed earth of the lodge floor, holding his temples and forehead in pain and disbelief. He raised his head, fighting for composure. "All of our beaver, Walking Feather? All of them?" Lyman's utter disappointment was registered in his tone.

"Eagle Tail says it is so. Let him speak."

Lyman looked at the Crow rider. "What can you tell me?"

Eagle Tail had a strong chiseled face and intelligent eyes; he had the long, almost noble nose characteristic of his tribe.

"The young man, the mixed-blood runner, did not come back when the sun was gone. After a sleep, some men and I followed his moccasin sign to the first stream of the safe beaver. We found lodges destroyed and beaver killed and not saved for pelts. By the fourth destroyed dam, the young runner was found dead, shot in the back, in the hips and part of his head shot. The sign at the destroyed beaver ponds was of four men, white men I know from the sign of the way they placed their feet, with riding horses and two for their packs."

Lyman raised his head to look at Walking Feather with moist, vacant eyes. "Skull!"

"With the three young demons I should have killed and taken scalps when they destroyed Grass Woman's maidenhood!" Walking Feather's voice was uncharacteristically bitter and vindictive, his mouth clamped and grim, his eyes boring in on Lyman's Such anger was foreign to Walking Feather and must have been embarrassing for him. Lyman's heart had turned to stone.

"You told me the doctor, Whitman, reported that they had been seen at the fort called Laramie. Why must all good things turn to dung, Jacob?"

"I should have killed Skull two years ago when I had the chance and spared his life," Lyman said.

Eagle Tail spoke up. "Men went out again before I was sent to ride to Walking Feather at this white man's camp.

They rode to all the streams to be sure. So that Walking Feather would know everything. All is destroyed. Most of the beaver killed. Any that were not killed were driven off. The dams, the lodges are no more. The water walks its old trail past broken dams and lodges and rotten dead beaver."

Lyman could not remember when he had suffered such anguish; his grand plan gone to ashes just as it was beginning to take hold, and amount to something that might pass for progress and strengthening the Indians' lot. He remembered Mark Whitman's impassioned words less than a week before: "Even now we are probably too late in preparing them."

This disaster set his plans back a year, if ever he could catch up again; the Indians had trusted him and somehow he'd failed them. As far as his alliance with the Crows was concerned, it was probably all over. "When did it happen, Eagle Tail?"

From his eyes, Lyman could see that the young Crow warrior had not had much contact with whites. He knew Lyman was a staunch friend of the Crows and that showed in the acceptance in his eyes, too.

"We brought the dead young mixed-blood to his mother for her grief and burial. It was a bad time. Five men went with the next sun to visit the saved beaver rivers. It was all the same everywhere. It has been eight or nine suns since the white men did the evil work."

Lyman looked hard at Walking Feather and shook his head again in disbelief over the gravity and the tragedy of the moment; and at that moment, with their mutual aspirations, hard work, cooperation, and persuasion against sometimes stubborn resistance gone up in smoke, he felt closer to Walking Feather than to any man he had ever known. They would be grandfathers to the same child, and it only strengthened the kinship. And they had worked hard together to create something decent and good. Now it was gone. His memory created the moments of watching the beaver and their kits splashing and sporting in the calm expanse of their dammed pond. At that moment, he would have killed the villainous and depraved Skull with his bare hands.

Walking Feather's voice broke a long and strained silence, but his wisdom spoke to Jake Lyman, sensing what was on his mind.

"The trail of judgment against evil is cold, Jacob. I do not speak for Griz Killer. I will not run out, vicious and snapping like a wild dog in the Hot Moon. I would waste precious suns tracking a blind trail. I might not return before the birth-squalls of our grandchild fill the birthing lodge. Surely No-Hair does this evil thing to set a trap for Griz Killer Lyman, and I think Walking Feather, too. The young devils remember my words of harsh judgment. No-Hair would know Walking Feather and Jacob and many others are here with the fur trading and he would not be pursued until his trail was very cold. No-Hair is as cunning as the wolf. If we find a trail after all these suns, it will be because No-Hair has laid a scent for the heedless who will fall into his snare."

"It's sure not a time for rash action," Jake agreed. "This is my fight with Skull. You and your people just happened to get in the way. It's me he wants. This is just a first message to let me know he's back and ready for a fight. All those beaver! All those months! All those hopes! Damn!"

Impulsively he jumped up.

"I have to think, Walking Feather. He may come after me. Or my family. I have to think what to do. I will come back and talk when I have thought of all this."

Standing, he pointed at Eagle Tail and made a sign of thanks. "You are a good man to ride so far and so hard to bring us this word."

"Griz Killer is a good man, too," Eagle Tail said. "To be such a friend of the Crows. You are spoken of well in our lodges."

Lyman's smile relaxed muscles stiff with the strain of his angry thoughts. "Such kindness takes much of the heaviness from my heart, Eagle Tail. We will speak again soon, Walking Feather."

Any brightness he felt in Eagle Tail's words deserted Lyman as he ducked out of the entry of Walking Feather's lodge, stepping into a sunlight that now seemed thin and bleak, in a hurry to find Rachel and talk over the distressing news; the darkness of the disaster spread like a gray cloud over him again as he walked.

WITH THE MISSIONARIES gone, the rendezvous scene switched to its old familiar mood of hilarity and wildness. Jugs came out and were passed, and the talk of men clustered at the fires raised to a new pitch. From the edge of the encampment, he could hear the barking reports of powder and ball as the rifle matches resumed in earnest.

As he trudged deep in thought back to his lodge, Lyman greeted and nodded to friends and acquaintances, but without enthusiasm. No point, he thought, in discussing his defeat with them. Few if any knew about, cared about, or even understood his obsession for his work with the Crows. Traders who had already encountered Crows grown shrewd with the knowledge spread by Lyman's and Walking Feather's alliance had greeted him with iciness bordering on open hostility. Bridger and the various company *bourgeois*—whom the mountain men called "booshways"—and factors seemed to have dismissed the project as having little hope of success or consequence. When the subject came up, they seemed to be more inclined to humor him and wish him well without serious interest or discussion of what he tried to accomplish. And why. He thanked God for small favors that at least they didn't try to drag him down or discourage the effort.

Little of that made any difference now, he thought glumly. His thoughts centered on Marcus Whitman, the one man who would have encouraging and consoling words, and positive thoughts for coping with the tragedy. But Whitman was three or four days away on the trail to Oregon.

Jake stooped to enter his lodge to find Rachel, Moon-That-Grows and Grass Woman clucking happily away in the Crow dialect about woman things like roosting hens.

With visitors in his home, Lyman tried to add a pleasant tone to his return.

"This looks like a happy group," he said, speaking to her in English. "Where are the parents-to-be?"

Rachel sought Jake's eyes, studied them, and perceived his somber mood. Still, she picked up his cue. "Daniel and Soft Wind went to watch the horse racing, they said." She spoke cheerfully, but looked apprehensively at her guests. "You've been to see Walking Feather. There's something wrong, isn't there, Jake."

"Not much escapes you, Mrs. Lyman."

"Because you have the inabilities of a trustworthy person to hide your true feelings. I've gotten where I can read your eyes and expression, Jacob, and at least sense your mood. You'll have a hard time hiding deceit from me."

He decided, under the circumstances, to continue the conversation in Crow. He looked at Moon-That-Grows and Grass Woman. "You will learn of it from Walking Feather. It's Skull's work. The man Walking Feather calls No-Hair. Our beaver preserves. All destroyed. Their dams and lodges. A Crow boy, a young man, they said who loved to run, a mixed-blood, found our enemies destroying the beaver and was killed."

Grass Woman gasped. "Andre!"

Moon-That-Grows looked at her daughter sternly. "Respect for the dead, child!" She turned to Lyman. "That is very sad. He was a good young man. Grass Woman and Soft Wind knew him well. Soft Wind, too, will be saddened. All the beaver, Jacob? All the streams?"

"All of them. All our work destroyed after all our talks

and arguments with the stubborn ones after the last fur encampment."

"I must go to my man! He will need me. Come, Grass Woman."

Moon-That-Grows got up and made ready to leave. Grass Woman gathered up some buckskin she was sewing on.

"A rider from your village came with the message. He is with Walking Feather now. Eagle Tail."

"My brother's son, a good man. My man will need me," Moon-That-Grows repeated. "Rachel, we shall speak together again."

The two Crow women bent to exit the door of the lodge.

Rachel came to Jake as quickly as the cover flap had dropped back in place behind them. He caught her in his arms.

"Jake, oh, Jake! I'm so sorry. After so much hope and work you've put into all this, to come to such a discouraging end. You're sure it was Skull?"

"The rider who came to Walking Feather saw it and was there when they found the dead boy. He described the tracks of four white men. We know Skull is back and apparently with the three that attacked Daniel and the girls last year. Only Skull would be vicious enough to do such a thing in revenge."

In her loving, comforting arms, in her soft, welcoming web of sympathy, Jake grit his teeth against anything as childish as tears; it was a devastating blow.

"It's hard when something comes along to shatter our dreams, isn't it, Jake?"

Her words struck deep responses within him. Lyman pulled back, resisting and rejecting the comfort of self-pity, and acknowledging the strength he gained from her. "Rachel! You're so kind, so sweet, so understanding. Yes, you're damned right about the shattered dreams. I feel looted, as broken inside as the beaver dams they pulled apart! But we're also strong, you and I." He realized even more how he gained inspiration and strength from her presence. He now wondered how he had survived the years before Rachel.

"This isn't the end of the world," he continued. "Walking Feather and his women are also strong. And we have new strength in our son and his wife and the coming grandchild we'll share with Walking Feather and Moon-That-Grows. Good will rise from all this wreckage. New resolve. I won't let that courageous Crow runner die in vain. We'll come back! Some way, we'll rise above all this. Even stronger."

"You spoke of Skull. I thought he was safely put away in the East. In prison."

"I didn't want to trouble you with so much going on that delighted you about being with Marcus and Narcissa. It seems Skull is back in the West. Mark knew a great deal. Skull escaped prison, killed two guards and, they're quite sure, a farmer in New York State. Somehow he's tied up with the three that attacked Daniel a year ago."

"We're all in danger again," Rachel said.

"True. But probably me more than others. I see his destruction of the beaver as taunting me to come after him for a fight to the finish that wasn't resolved two years ago!"

Her eyes bored into his. "So I suppose you're going after him."

He chuckled, but with a sardonic tone. "That, I'm afraid, was the old Jake Lyman. No, Walking Feather's wisdom prevails. And I've tried to think what sort of consoling but sage advice Mark Whitman would have for me. No, my dear, we'll do the safe thing and the thing Skull least expects. He'll be sure I'll get hot on his trail. Instead we'll go about things as though we had no idea he was involved. That'll put the shoe on the other foot. *He's* the one, Rachel, who'll be driven to distraction! Meanwhile, we'll all have to keep foremost in our minds that old warning about watching our backtrail. Skull's been out of this country two years, so knows little of our movements. He probably remembers where our cabin is; that's about all. We'll just keep watchful for him as we do for the threat of bears or catamounts when we're out."

"That's a bit scary, but preferable to having you out on the trail for revenge again."

"So that's the gist of my plan. But somehow I'm not overly worried. I have a hunch that Skull and his boys headed north or east. He's a heavy drinker and I don't doubt they are, too. They'll want to be near a source of their whiskey, like Fort Laramie or one of the better river posts along the Missouri. They'll likely stick close to one with a fairly constant flow of Indians coming to trade where there'll be some of the low camp-following squaws, another needed commodity of their kind. Was I to take out after them, I'd most likely head for Fort Union on the upper Missouri. Skull will probably be slow getting there, doubling back once in a while to see if Griz Killer is on his trail. And I hope it perplexes the hell out of him when I don't show up!"

"I'm proud of you for curbing your anger, Jacob."

"We always say there's more than one way to skin a cat. I'm tickled how I'll have Skull stewing in his own broth!"

Footsteps outside the lodge stopped near their entry and the flap raised as Daniel and Soft Wind stepped in. Lyman's daughter-in-law had the glowing look of a young mother-to-be, her rich and clear dusky complexion lightly flushed from their walk, her eyes and her expression radiant with optimism and joy.

Her presence with Daniel beside her, every inch of him now righteous and responsible, sent feelings of great elation through Lyman—the best he'd felt all day.

Things—suddenly—didn't look all that grim.

"Daniel," he said. "Could you and I take a little walk and leave your wife for a few moments with Mother? Some things have come up that I need to talk over with you. Rachel, maybe you can explain to Soft Wind. Come on, Dan!"

*   *   *

"I KNOW YOU, Jacob. It must be hard not to want to get on Skull's trail right now and even the score," Daniel said as they wended their way back to the lodge after the long walk in which Jake explained the disaster. "Get it straight that I owe Skull nothing. If you wanted to start out after him right now, you'd have trouble keeping me home. I know what kind of person Skull was trying to make of me. I don't hold pleasant thoughts, Jacob. I've also got a score to settle with those three you say are running with him. What they did to my wife and her sister a year ago! I've got my own reasons for vengeance. Now this thing they did, this destruction wronged and deeply hurt both my new fathers—you and Walking Feather. That's enough for me to start after them myself. And I would!"

Walking beside him, Lyman looked at Daniel's eyes; the sure determination of his words was there. Jake knew that Daniel England had become a man of his word.

"I think we're going to do enough mischief to Skull simply by *not* tracking him down for revenge," Lyman said. "I'm sure he was laying a trap for me. I was supposed to stumble into it as I chased him all fired up." He smiled at his son. "But that was the old Jake Lyman."

"So it's done and over with unless he shows up around here. I'm glad we all can see it that way." Daniel smiled back.

"As far as I'm concerned, it is. He just may come back to bring us more trouble, so we have to be on our guard."

"He'll be seen if he comes around here. We have lots of friends in this country. Word will get to us in time, Jake." It was the first time Daniel had used Lyman's nickname and he let it pass, pleased that they had forged such a close bond.

"Before this bad news today," Daniel went on, "I had something I needed to speak with you about. This gives me the chance."

Lyman's face knit with apprehension; it didn't sound good. "And that is?"

"I don't know exactly how to bring it up with you. Try to understand. I've done a lot of thinking. I'm soon going to be a father. Soft Wind and I have talked much. She wants our child to have an American name."

"Well, that's your right as the parents. I'm sure Walking Feather will understand."

"But you don't, father," Daniel said, almost protesting. "It's the last name. Do you have any objection if Soft Wind and I take the name Lyman?"

Jake was almost overwhelmed with emotion. First to be devastated with Skull's depraved attack; now Daniel wanted to take his name. His heart soared; Daniel had called him father. "Of course, son," he said, almost stammering. "You don't know how proud that makes me."

"Mother has taken your name. And, well, I feel toward you as she does. And we feel—Mother and I—the same about my real father. He will always be honored in our hearts, but we have new lives now. A new future. We're Lymans now!"

"Now I'm the one that's honored," Jake said, still reeling inside as all this hit him so unexpectedly. "And, Dan, since I'm not your real father, it's all right if you call me Jake. But maybe not around your mother, or among those who might not understand the familiarity. Can we do that?"

Daniel smiled at him and to Lyman it was a heart-warming smile; Skull's dirty work did not seem nearly as monumental now. He and Walking Feather could start afresh with new beaver streams, and keep more careful watch. Nothing was more important than the closeness he had just now with his son.

"Of course I understand, and that's good to know. There's one more thing I wanted us to speak of, Jake."

Lyman looked at his new son, his expression telling him to proceed.

"The child's name. If it's a girl, we haven't come up with anything, but we'll probably decide on a name that's a little Indian and a little American. Acceptable either way."

"Possible, I guess," Lyman agreed.

"If it's a boy, we have a name."

"And . . .?"

"Edwin Jacob Lyman!"

1837

Chapter Twenty

No-Hair Skull and Will Dooley sat in the full, bland, late-June sunlight of the levee outside Fort Union, nursing large cups of trader's whiskey, watching the wide, placid Missouri flow gently down the endless miles toward St. Louis, neither particularly suited to appreciate the pleasant combination of restful view, warm sunshine, and fresh air.

They simply sat out the intolerable hours, soothing their prickly nerves with hootch, waiting for the steamboat.

A rider coming from the south along the river the day before had reported sighting the American Fur Company steamer, *St. Peters*, slowly chugging its way upstream toward Fort Union.

They couldn't know the special brand of hellish pestilence the boat's cargo had unloaded downstream at Fort Clark—a devil's blight that was to virtually destroy the Mandan and the Minnetaree Indian tribes.

"Reckon Jack and Luke gonna be on the boat, Skull?" Will Dooley pulled his snout out of his whiskey cup long enough to speak.

Skull looked at his companion impatiently. Over the past year, he'd become more and more convinced of the nincompoop mentality he'd brought back with him into the western territories.

Still, Skull figured, he could have done worse in finding willing stooges; they made his life easy with their eagerness

183

to serve. A year ago, his trio of lackeys had done most of the dirty work in tearing down the hated Lyman's precious beaver preserve. When it came to killing the Indian kid who'd caught them red-handed, they quickly obeyed Skull's orders to fire on the fleeing lad, each one scoring a hit. Jack Butler, who'd become Skull's second-in-command, even blew off part of the little bastard's head.

Leaving a trail a one-eyed idiot could follow in hopes Lyman would come charging after them, Skull pointed them north to the high Missouri country, while en route they put under a few solitary trappers for their plews and possibles, adding to their coin of the fur-trade realm by seeking out and looting buried caches of cured and packed beaver pelts.

Still, he was rankled and short-tempered that his planned pursuit by Griz-Killer Lyman hadn't borne fruit. Skull's old boss, Thomas Penn, had told him how easily Lyman had been duped once to blunder into a trap of Penn's design. It was unlike Griz Killer not to make some effort at revenge.

"Hell if I know Dooley," Skull said tiredly. "They, by God, better be. The little son-a-bitches wintered-over in Sa'nt Louie selling our beaver for better money than they give up here and getting our fixin's and our whiskey at Sa'nt Louie prices, not how we're gouged by these blasted rivermud traders! Them two had their fill of sweet waterfront white girls, you can bet. Them little Frenchies back there are about the best a man'll find." Skull studied the water wistfully.

"All we got," he added, "are these damned squaws layin' there like a side of dead meat thinking only of the handful of beads we promised 'em. Cuffin' 'em around don't seem to liven 'em up any either. I'd almost as leave poke it into a statue!"

Dooley finished his whiskey and swiped a sleeve across his mouth. "Heard the trader tellin' that this un'll be the last boat of the season. Water's gettin' low an' they'll ride up on ever' gravel bar twixt here an' Westport Landin'."

"Then they better by God get here," Skull said impatiently, almost as if finishing Dooley's statement for him. "Else when I catch up to 'em, I'll lift some hair and skin their legs for leggins and make tobacco pokes out of their sacks!"

Dooley, feeling his cargo of morning whiskey on an empty stomach, stared at Skull in wide-eyed disbelief. Still, he knew Skull was not a man to be crossed.

As if to punctuate Skull's threat, floating around the river's bend below the fort, came the hoarse but shrill and drawn out scream of the *St. Peters'* steam whistle, slicing the still and warm morning air like a knife.

Equally muted by distance and the land and water barrier of the bend came the whuff of steam-driven pistons, the stroking squeal of driving rods, and the rhythmic slap and splash of a pair of side-mounted paddlewheels.

As they watched, with cheering, yelling Indians, traders, and trappers alike pounding toward the levee from the fort and the surrounding Indian camps, the glistening white prow, low almost to the point of shipping water, slowly nosed around the bend. Steamboat sounds rose stronger to the ear now with nothing to impede them.

From the screen of trees of the bend, the Texas deck edged into view, surmounted by the sparkling-white and many-windowed wheelhouse and backed by the great black flared and fluted stacks turning the air over them black with dense wood-smoke; throngs now filling the levee around Skull and Dooley could see the steamer's master prominent at his post in his visored black cap hovering over the great wheel making steering corrections ever so carefully as the great white and gleaming brass low-slung monster made its approach.

A giant muscular Negro in nondescript slave clothing stood at the port side of the prow clutching a massive hawser ready to make the first securing of the boat to a deep-sunk piling at water's edge.

As the struggling steamer quartered toward the Fort Union levee, the same side of the low-slung cargo deck was crowded with trappers in buckskins and company men in combinations of buckskin and St. Louis-styled raiment, and here and there a man of culture in tailored finery spinning a glowing cheroot in his fingers.

Skull and Dooley searched in vain for a sight of Butler and Farmer among those on the deck. They looked almost straight across at the passengers as the master ordered the paddlewheel reversed to brake the boat's forward thrust. Again the master reached for the whistle cord and the shrill eruption of steam blasted the ears of bystander and passenger alike.

"Keep those people back!" came a shout from the cargo deck. "Keep 'em Injuns back! We got the sickness aboard!"

A few of the whites who understood, particularly company men and traders, hopelessly outnumbered, made feeble attempts to hold back the throngs of happily eager, cackling, crowing, and grinning Indians as they crowded forward to see what manner of goods the Canoe-That-Walks had brought them.

"Keep 'em back!" demanded the stern voice of a crewman on deck. "We got smallpox!"

A voice ashore rose in Assiniboine tongue. "Bad sickness!"

Still the Indians surged forward.

"Hold 'em back," came the voice from the deck again. "We got to drop the ramp and get these passengers off!"

The boat's great wide walkway of planks stood hinged and upright against the superstructure ready to be lowered to the levee by a pair of sturdy cables supported by pulleys.

The traders and company men moved among the Indians closest to the boat, striving hard to shoo them away. Like a hill of sand, for every small group they pushed back, others sidled forward elsewhere.

"Ah, hell!" a trader shrieked. "Bad sickness," he shouted in Indian tongue. "Make way!"

An Indian voice rose loud in protest from the crowd. "Another white man trick to cheat and rob us!"

From the mob of passengers on deck, another strident voice was raised. "Come on! Lower the gawdam gangplank. I want off this stinking tub!"

"Yeah!" someone else bellered.

"Keep them Injuns back," the crewman's voice shouted.

Another black laborer appeared on the Texas deck to free the latch holding the upright gangway in place. With the squeal of a racheted windlass somewhere, the ramp cranked down, like a castle drawbridge, to span the moat between land and deck.

The boat's cargo master preceded the passengers to meet some of the traders, struggling to get to the ramp among the excited Indians.

"I don't believe it'll be bad, Joseph," the boatman declared, recognizing a trader. Skull and Dooley stood close enough to hear. "A couple of men on board are down with the smallpox. But they been vaccinated and hain't had bad cases. Down to Fort Clark, though, where we tied up on the fifteenth to drop off their freight, a damn Mandan got on board and stole a blanket from a sick man. Everyone was jumpy for a while. Time we left there was no reports of sickness. So it'll all prob'ly be all right."

"You should've tied up downstream and fumigated everything, 'specially the cargo, Len."

"No time for that. On top of that, we didn't think about it. We're running a tight schedule as it is, Joseph. We'll have to unload and turn about right smart 'fore the depth drops any lower. We scraped bottom a few times comin' up as it was. River's as low this year as I've seen. In another week, we probably wouldn't be able to get out of here 'til Fall. And you know how they'd raise hell about that in Sa'nt Louie!"

Skull's attention was diverted to the stream of passengers off the boat, scanning every face for Butler and Farmer. He hailed the last man off the boat.

"See here, you," Skull called, boldly approaching the man. "A couple of more passengers we're looking for.

Named Butler and Farmer. Seen 'em? Heard of 'em?"

"Nobody by them names on the manifest or I'd've known. I'm what they call the purser this trip. Responsible for such as that."

"Those two they said are down with the pox? Know them?"

"Couple of crewmen. One's a company man, the other's a darky. But they both been vaccinated an' don't have bad cases. We jes' don't want to expose these heathen Indian. Gittin' 'em all sick ain't good for business, if ya know what I mean."

Without so much as acknowledging the man's information, Skull turned angrily to Dooley.

"They didn't make the boat! Damn!"

Dooley's face beamed with the first bright idea he'd had in years. "What if they took our money and run?"

Realization dawned on Skull. "Why those double-crossin' son-a-bitches! Hell, I bet we sent two-hundred dollars worth of plews with those back-stabbin' bastards!"

Skull's face, to the dome of his gleaming plate, turned red with fury. Fired with rage, he turned on the only connection he had with the two thieves, Will Dooley.

"You know 'em better than I do, dammit! Would Butler pull a trick like that?"

"Hell, Skull, Jack Butler'd put his mother to work in a whorehouse if he thought he could make a dollar."

"Farmer go along with it?"

"They're alike as peas in a pod."

"Why the hell didn't you tell me?"

"First off, you didn't ask me. Besides, I'd not've told you with them standin' right there!"

"Damn! I've half a mind to cash in what plews we pulled together since they left last fall and buy me a ticket on that steamer to Sa'nt Louie and go on the prowl for that pair."

"Take me, too. I don't want to be up here alone!" Will Dooley was a man who couldn't stomach loneliness.

"Ah, you're a goddam misfit just like those other two. Come on! I still got a jug near full back in the lodge."

*   *   *

WELL AFTER DARK, their legs rubbery and their heads foggy and lolling on their necks, Skull and Dooley dragged themselves out of their cluttered lodge and went on the prowl of the Indian camp virtually on three sides of Fort Union. They'd not eaten all day, but the whiskey had sharpened appetites for something that required other forms of appeasement: Girls.

Copious amounts of whiskey all day had blunted Skull's rage at being taken in by Farmer and Butler; this night he was uncommonly good-natured.

In the dark ahead of them they heard approaching giggles and girlish Indian talk. Dooley chuckled. "Yonder comes a couple of leetle ones, Skull," he said softly and slurring. "Let's git 'em!"

"Long as they're young, Will, poontang's poontang," Skull agreed.

"Ahhh!" Dooley murmured, expectantly. "I got sumthin' good for 'em."

"One of them, " Skull corrected drunkenly.

"Yes, marster," Dooley agreed. "Maybe when we git th'ough fist whack, Skull, we'd oughtta swap."

"You ain't man enough," Skull challenged.

"Just for that, I'll prove it," Dooley promised, being unusually bold with the man he owed allegiance to.

Two short, blanket-draped figures emerged out of the dark ahead of them.

Dooley spoke up. "Hoka-hey!"

The two Indian girls stopped, shy and tittering, watching the white men as if awaiting the invitation.

In the dark but close enough that the girls could see, Skull made the sign of what they were after and that the two men had a lodge. Dooley groped in a pouch at his waist and fished out a handful of trade beads. Cupping them in both hands he shook them until they rattled. The girls tittered again and looked at each other grinning and made a sign at Skull that they would go.

Skull caught one by the arm and jerked her toward him and, grabbing her buttocks, thrust himself rudely against her, gyrating his hips. She shrieked in Indian gaiety and pulled away slightly, cackling. She thrust out her hand to give his hard, hidden lump several quick, loving strokes, mumbling Indian words of promise.

Dooley, still reeling in the dark, got one arm around the other girl's waist, and extended his arm and hand downward. "Damn," he exclaimed, "how gawdam down is this gawdam dress?" He found its end near her ankles and slid his hand up, hiking the skirt. His girl laughed like she was being tickled.

They both were drunk, too.

SOME TIME LATER, in the dim light of a bed of coals in the center of their lodge floor, a pleasantly mellow and but only partly gratified Skull called out in the dimness of the lodge to his companion. "Hey, Dooley!"

Out of the dark, Dooley responded: "Huh?"

"We going to swap?"

"Aw, no. No more. No more for me. I gotta sleep!"

"Damn tadpoles! Then crawl out of the gawdam way and let a real man go to work."

Beneath Dooley, the Indian girl, understanding, protested, saying she'd given enough for the beads she was promised. "Another man, more beads!" she insisted.

Dooley dragged himself off of her and crawled to another part of the lodge and slumped in a heap.

Skull stood tall over his first conquest and took the few steps to where Dooley's girl made as if to get up and leave. Skull leaned down, grabbed her shoulders and rudely shoved her back prone.

"You got to answer to the chief before you get them beads," he growled at her, moving into position over her.

An unburned length of wood at the edge of the fire took flame like a torch, filling the lodge with light.

Skull looked at the girl as he knelt over her, poised for the thrust.

"Hey! Wait a minute! That's a brand new blanket you got!" Skull paused in shocked realization. "Ain't been no brand new blankets at Fort Union since last season. That came up on the boat today! Dooley!"

Skull's lodge companion was dead to the world.

"Where'd you get it?" he demanded of the girl.

Simpering, she shrunk down into the soft and new green Hudson's Bay point blanket, her eyes wide in horror at Skull's deadly sinister and hideous death's-head face in the garish, flickering firelight.

Furious, Skull plowed a fist into the girl's mouth, bringing a shriek of horror and terror; the other girl, screaming and clutching her own new blanket, leaped to her feet to escape and disappear out the lodge opening.

Under him, in Skull's total power, Dooley's girl brought her hands up in protection as Skull gestured with another fist ready to slam into her face.

"Where'd you get the blanket?! Or so help me I'll make you ugly the rest of your life!"

She muttered something softly.

"Say again! I didn't hear you." He shoved the knuckles of his balled fist to grind harshly against her chin. "I'll open up your gawdam head!"

The terrified girl spoke the words again, this time louder and more distinct.

Skull leaped up in horror. "Holy . . . ! Dooley! These two squaws we got went and bedded crewmen off the gawdam boat this evenin' before us! Dooley! Smallpox! Dammit! They prob'ly give us the smallpox!"

* * *

TWO OR THREE days later, several of the numerous squaws hanging around the fort the day the *St. Peters* arrived, died violent deaths from smallpox, the first spark of the wildfire that decimated Indians in the vicinity of Fort Union. Farther downstream at Fort Clark, among the Mandans and the Minnetarees exposed to white man's maladies, the plague began to run like a mighty, ferocious tide. Thousands—perhaps tens of thousands—died. Death became so prevalent that traditional burial was impossible. Bodies were thrown in wholesale lots off cliffs. The stench around riverfront posts and stricken Indian camps was intolerable.

The Mandan tribe, once proud and powerful, counted a mere thirty-three survivors. The Minnetarees suffered similar decimation. The equally proud but vicious Blackfeet were brought to their knees. Crows, Aricaras, Assiniboines, all were severely hit. When the plague descended on a lodge, husband executed wife and then committed suicide before enduring the brief but intolerable agonies. Friends made similar pacts.

A suffocating heat settled over the land to make the suffering even more ghastly. With so much random death, wolves in great numbers prowled village perimeters, feasting on bodies dragged out and abandoned.

European nobleman Prince Maximilian of Weid, touring the American West, observed the firestorm of epidemic. He wrote:

"The destroying angel has visited the unfortunate sons of the wilderness with terrors never before known, and has converted the extensive hunting grounds, as well as the peaceful settlements of these tribes, into desolate and boundless cemeteries . . . the warlike spirit which but lately animated the several Indian tribes, and but a few months ago gave reason to apprehend the breaking out of a sanguinary war, is broken. The mighty warriors are now prey of the greedy wolves, and the few survivors, in utter despair, throw themselves on the pity of the whites, who, however, can do little for them. The vast preparations for the protection of the western frontier are superfluous; another arm has undertaken the defense of the white inhabitants of the frontier; and the funeral torch, that lights the red man to his dreary grave, has become the auspicious star of the advancing settler and the roving trader of the white race."

FOUR DAYS AFTER the arrival of the steamer *St. Peters* at Fort Union, Skull awoke with a monstrous headache, lethargy, and agony in his muscles and bones. He wearily reassured himself he'd gotten a batch of bad whiskey. He figured to sleep it off for a day in his and Will Dooley's lodge.

Late in the afternoon Dooley, who'd gone to swap some beaver pelts for another whiskey jug, dragged himself into the lodge and shook Skull awake. "Skull! Wake up. I ain't feelin' so good."

Skull awoke groggy with new and great pain centering in his chest and belly to confront a face over him peppered with swollen red splotches. Dooley's eyes were bleary and bloodshot.

"Hey, Skull," Dooley said. "You don't look so good neither. Your face is all broke out with pimples. Big uns!"

1839

Chapter Twenty-One

IT HAD BEEN A QUIET, PLEASANT SUMMER ON JAKE LYMAN'S mountain.

In mid-August, with balmy days and crisp nights that foretold the Moon of Dropping Leaves, a stranger, a large man on a strong horse, toiled uphill from the river toward the giant clearing on the mountain flat that marked the homesite of Lyman's upgraded and expanded cabin-home.

His face and his mouth both were grim-set, near frozen expressions that cloaked the expansive, fun-loving rascal that was Jim Bridger.

The horse struggled against the steeps, carrying the heavy load of big man and some of his possibles, following a well-marked trail from the river. He also clutched the lead rope of a horse bearing a well-loaded crude sawbuck pack-saddle; Jim Bridger was on a long trip, tracking down old friends over this, the most singular summer of his life.

Horse and man broke from the slope to crest a great flat space, once heavily fortified, now randomly cleared with but scattered great monarchs of pine and fir spared to provide shade, serenity and gentle wind symphonies in Lyman's heaven.

Jake Lyman materialized like a ghost from behind one of the trees, carrying at the ready the old familiar Hawken big-bore rifle that had earned him the legendary "Griz Killer" nickname.

Bridger grinned inwardly; Jake had heard him coming and, seasoned hivernant that he was, had a good look at the stranger before showing up out in the open. "Jim Bridger!" Lyman exclaimed. "What're you doing in these parts?"

In Bridger's eyes, Jake Lyman hadn't changed much from the good-looking, finely muscled porkeater he'd first known way back in 1822 when both had responded to Andy Henry and Bill Ashley's *Missouri Republican* advertisement for a hundred "enterprising young men . . . to ascend the Missouri river to its source" headed for, as they'd been told, a region that abounded in a "wealth of furs not surpassed by the mines of Peru." Bridger and Lyman had been told they'd explore and trap all "the streams on both sides of the mountains in that region and would very likely penetrate to the mouth of the Columbia!"

In the years since, together and separate, he and Jake Lyman had seen most of it. Bridger, with his itchy foot, maybe broke more trails, found more passes and left his name on more places on the land than Jake or any other of his peers. Bridger also respected and envied Jake above a great many others as a steady, reliable trapper content to limit his range, trap well and productively, keep to himself mostly—but as staunch a friend as a man would want—and trade in beaver plews properly skinned and cleaned, and carefully cured and packed.

"I'll put it to you bluntly, Jake, what I'm doing here. This here's the first summer since '24 there'll be no rendezvous. That sort of eats at a man. The bottom's dropped for good and all out of the bucket we thought back in them first days we could never drain. I suppose in such a season as this in a man's life when the dancing and the delights of his days are behind him, he needs to go seek out people, friends, men he's lived and caroused and fought side by side with and survived and been to the mountain with. Like you."

Jake dropped the Hawken's butt to the ground and grinned up at Bridger, careful not to have the grin taken as making light of the deep sentiment and gravity of Jim's words. Bridger, he knew, was two or three years younger than he, but their times in the mountains and along the streams had seasoned them differently. Jim had taken on his role of legend as the old man of the mountains as his face, his form, and his bearing had adjusted to the mold. Jim Bridger had come to fit his image.

"That bein' the case, Mr. Bridger, get down, stretch your legs, ease your cramps, and stay a few days. We'll eat and we'll talk."

Walking toward the imposing log house still, in these easier times, outfitted and secure for defense, Bridger led his horse while Jake took the pack horse's lead rope.

"Where's your boy these days, Jake?"

"He's here, yonder south along the river about a quarter-mile. His own place with Soft Wind, his wife, Walking Feather's daughter."

Lyman beamed with pride at Bridger. "I've a two-year-old grandson now, Jim. Edwin Jacob Lyman. He's a humdinger! We built a fine cabin over there, Dan and I. A few paces away, through the woods, Dan keeps a right proper Crow lodge for Moon-that-Grows. She's been here with us since she lost Walking Feather and Grass Woman, their other daughter, in the scourge of '37."

"I been wanting to speak with you of that, too, Jake."

Lyman's features darkened. "It was as bad a blow as I've ever been hit with. The birth of little Eddie was the knot that bound us all together as a family. We were so looking forward to shinin' times. Walking Feather never saw the baby." Lyman bit his lip in a backwash of residual grief.

As they approached the cabin, the door swung open and, with face alight, Rachel emerged.

"Jim Bridger!" she called. "As I live and breathe!"

"Rachel Lyman! It's been a while. Like always, the sight

of you is balm for these sick old eyes. You got a welcome embrace for an old brown bear?"

"If you hadn't asked, I would have!" Rachel exclaimed happily, throwing herself at Bridger's outstretched arms.

After they'd hugged, Bridger stepped back, still clutching Rachel's forearms fondly, looking deeply into her eyes.

"Doc Whitman's Angel of Bellevue! I swear, you grow prettier by the day, Mrs. Lyman."

"And time's not dimmed your voice of the charmer, Mr. Bridger. Are you hungry?"

"I always preserve a corner of my paunch for the right opportunity. As I remember, you had good upbringing in your mother's kitchen and then learned a sight more among our red brethren about the proper preparin' of wild game."

"Come in," she said.

As they entered the spacious, inviting lodge room of the Lyman's big cabin, Jake spoke up. "We'll have us a little to tide us over for now, Jim. These hills are full of deer and elk. We'll hunt this afternoon and have us a fine feast on fresh meat this night."

"Maybe wander by and see your boy and his young-un. I mean to extend my sympathy to Moon-that-Grows and Soft Wind. I know I'm two years late, but decency is never out of place. Who's the boy favor?"

"Daniel," Rachel blurted.

"Walking Feather," Jake said at the same time. "Little Eddy has the fine features of the Crow and a rich cast of skin. If there's any good looks on the white side of his blood, and Rachel and Dan have plenty, the boy got the best of that!"

"But what about you, Jake," Bridger started. "Oh, forgive me. I plumb forgot. He's not of your blood."

"But he'll be of Jake's influence. It's what's inside a person that counts."

"Couldn't've said it better myself," Bridger observed. "I've a mixed-blood child myself. Little Mary Ann. Speaking of influence, I taken steps to have her proper brought up, something I in my life won't be able to do. I've arranged to have her live with Doc and Narcissa Whitman at their mission in the Oregon country. Joe Meek's in the same situation with little Helen Mar. She's half Nez Perce anyway. You know Joe and his ways, Jake. Named the child after somebody he'd read about, he said, in a book by some Miss Porter called *Scottish Chiefs*. We taken the girls there to learn proper ways under Miz Whitman."

Jim was thoughtful for a long moment. "S'pose you heard about losing their child."

Jake looked at Rachel. "We heard. But no details."

Bridger's eyes grew moist. "Wa'nt but a tad older'n that boy of young Dan'l's. Here—this is August; in June, it was. A Sunday. Worse day of the week for such a thing for those fine, upstanding, religious people. They got occupied with other things and the little girl strayed to the river and that was it."

"Oh, Jake!" Copious tears spilled down Rachel's cheeks.

"I must write Mark and Narcissa," Lyman said softly. "Such a tragedy! Mark and Narcissa must be devastated!"

"They're strong people," Bridger continued. "Faith. I never knew it the way they do. Wish sometimes I did. They found her body right off in the water and did what they could to revive her. But it was too late."

"Jake, we must be sure Soft Wind keeps Eddy away from the river!"

"Jim and I mean to stop there on our hunt, Rachel. I'll bring it up with Dan and Soft Wind."

HOURS LATER, JAKE and Jim, transporting a fine young buck deer with just the start of spikes in his forehead, properly bled and gutted, paused for a breather on a grand hillside of random rocks and tall, magnificently needled trees reaching their tapered crowns toward the sun. It was almost dark in their meshed-limb shade.

"I s'pose Walking Feather's dying wrote the last line on your grand plan to work with the Indians, Jake."

"At least as far as the beaver preserves were concerned. His death and Skull's destruction of our first year's work kind of took the heart out of me for it."

"But your heart was good, Jake. That's what mattered."

"Daniel and Soft Wind make trips back to Crow country to keep her close to her people. They work with many of them on their English. When Eddy is older, they'll keep him in touch with both sides of where he comes from."

"Can't help but make him a stronger man. He'll have his troubles as a mixed blood, but knowing and growing strong in the best of both worlds can't but make him a man to survive it."

"It was just as well I didn't take out after Skull when he tore up our preserves that way. Dan found out that Skull was among the first to die when the smallpox hit Fort Union."

"One of those three rapscallions died with him."

"Dan heard it was Dooley. Never saw hide nor hair of the others, Butler and Farmer. They must've gotten away scot-free."

"You ain't up on the news from down below. It was a year ago. In Sa'nt Louie. A hoss that knew them two it was that told me. Jack Butler got his guts opened in a saloon knife fight. Mouthy little bastard prob'ly had it coming. Farmer disappeared."

"Good riddance," Lyman observed.

"So you lost Walking Feather and your dream. The smallpox to my way of thinking was the kiss of death for us beaver men, too. Trading with the Indians went to hell in a handbasket overnight. Several of the tribes all but wiped out. Blackfeet that two weeks before was after your scalp and thirsty for your blood comin' in beggin' and wailin' for the white man's help. Lord, but it was pitiful! Anybody that'd ever fought 'em like we did, would have to own up to that! But the whites had nothing to offer but merciful thoughts. Crows brought to their knees, too. The last straw, Jake. It broke the back of our trade, no two ways about it."

"You're probably right. Trapping's been on thin ice for years, Jim. The smallpox only hastened the inevitable."

"Well, it's all over, Jake. The shinin' times. Beaver hit rock bottom, the big companies gone bust, whites comin' in droves for California and Oregon. Sodbusters runnin' furrows out on the grasslands. Buffalo with no place to go where there ain't rifles. We'll never see the old days again. The bloom's withered and dead, that's all there is to it. But warn't the country beautiful to behold in those days?!"

"Mark Whitman once remarked that the only thing that's inevitable is change."

"Waugh! It was so good, Jake. Why did it have to change? Why do the good things turn to dung?"

"Huh!" Lyman grunted. "Walking Feather said the very same thing when our preserves were destroyed! Whitman called it the long and sometimes dark journey toward the light. It's life, Jim."

Bridger brightened. "At least, Jake, we saw it at its finest. They was shinin' times, wa'n't they?!"

Epilogue

THE SEVERAL QUESTS OF DR. MARCUS WHITMAN AND Narcissa Whitman to introduce what, in their dedicated, caring and well-intentioned minds, were the best they had to offer by way of introduction to the white man's culture, religion and care to the tribes of the northwest appear to have been perpetually star-crossed.

The bulk of the Cayuse Indians under their purview were neither cooperative nor malleable. Rev. Henry Spalding's spiteful and divisive behavior continued to distress and divide. The seeds of dissension were many and often subtle and too involved for this discussion.

Eastbound reports of the bickering and poor progress came to a head with a September, 1842, letter from the American Board of Foreign Missions of the Presbyterian Church—sponsors of the Whitman and Spalding missions. The board ordered the closing of two of its missions, the recalling of several missionaries, and reassignment for the Whitmans.

Deeply troubled by the letter, Dr. Whitman decided to go east in person to plead the case for the threatened missions before the board. As ill-advised as such an ambitious trip was in the dead of winter, he set out October 3, 1842, with two companions, an Indian and a white guide. Persuaded to detour south because of rumors of Indian unrest—if not the bitter cold and deep snows, the Whitman party dipped as far south as Santa Fe, New Mexico, before swinging north to Bent's Old Fort on the Arkansas River in south central Colorado. He reached Westport, Missouri, in February, and continued to hasten east. He visited Washington, D.C., and New York City before going by boat to Boston. There, his monumental and arduous trip was a success, as the board was persuaded to rescind its earlier decrees.

Heading West in April, 1843, Whitman joined a caravan of roughly a thousand immigrants at Independence, Missouri, the largest yet to assemble for the trip to Oregon. He arrived home in September, five days shy of a year since his departure.

As with the cholera that infected most of Fontenelle's crewmen in 1835, and the shocking devastation of the 1837 smallpox epidemic among the Indian tribes of the upper Missouri, the massacre of Marcus and Narcissa Whitman at their Waiilatpu mission complex on November 29, 1847, at the hands of malcontent Cayuse was the result of white man's disease rampant among susceptible Indians.

The origins of the uprising, however, were as many and varied as the earlier dissension among the missionaries. The Cayuse observed bitterly that more and more the Whitman mission had become a warm and welcoming waystation and hostelry for the flood of white immigrants over the Oregon Trail, rather than the place of solace, healing and guidance for the Cayuse that it had been for many years.

Autumn of 1847 brought a wagon train infected with measles; the malady spread to the Cayuse and, as with the smallpox epidemic farther east along the upper Missouri ten years earlier, it ran rampant among the vulnerable Indians. Though Marcus Whitman exhausted every medical means at his disposal to help, cure and to comfort, half the tribe died within two months. Halfbreeds Joe Lewis and Nicholas Finley fed the flames of superstition and fear, alleging that Whitman was either not doing enough, was withholding the cure, or was openly poisoning them.

Despite the fact that residents at the mission were also stricken—both Mary Ann Bridger and Helen Mar Meek were bedridden with measles—the Cayuse and the half-breeds plotted revenge.

When they rose up that fearful and fateful November day in 1847, Dr. Whitman was killed first—tomahawked. Narcissa, herself ill and carried from the house on a couch, was brutally shot to death sometime later. In all, thirteen of the nearly fifty-five residents of the mission were massacred.

Helen Mar Meek and Mary Ann Bridger were among the survivors.